Praise for Bonnie Dee and Marie Treanor's *Demon Lover*

"A beautiful twist to the classic tale of Rumpelstiltskin. Gwyneth and the demon who helps her is written with such intensity it pulls at your heart strings. Brilliant, I was unable to put the book down."

~ *Sensual Reads*

"This was a wonderful adult adaptation of a well-known fairytale. I enjoyed the premise and the love scenes were smoking hot. Our demon lover was so complex; one minute ruthless in his pursuit and then so compassionate."

~ *The Romance Studio*

"The pacing of the story was a steady one and the relationship between Gwyneth and Ragnorak didn't feel rushed. Sex in this story was actually written quite sweetly, and was used to emphasize intimacy."

~ *JERR, L. Yay*

"This is a fast paced story that will have you scrolling the pages to see what will happen next. Ragnorak is a drool-worthy hero and Gwyneth is more than his match."

~ *Love Romances*

Look for these titles by *Bonnie Dee*

Now Available

Finding Home (with Lauren Baker)
Evolving Man
Blackberry Pie
Opposites Attract
Perfecting Amanda
The Valentine Effect
The Countess Takes a Lover
The Final Act
Empath
The Countess Lends a Hand
Butterfly Unpinned (with Laura Bacchi)
The Thief and the Desert Flower
Star Flyer
Magical Menages: Shifters' Captive
Magical Menages: Vampires' Consort

Fairytale Fantasies Series
Cinderella Unmasked (with Marie Treanor)
Demon Lover (with Marie Treanor)
Awakening Beauty (with Marie Treanor)

Print Anthologies
Midsummer Night's Steam: Heat Wave
Gifted
Strangers in the Night

Look for these titles by *Marie Treanor*

Now Available

Killing Joe
Gothic Dragon
Ariadne's Thread
The Devil and Via
Queen's Gambit
Requiem for Rab

Fairytale Fantasies Series
Cinderella Unmasked (with Bonnie Dee)
Demon Lover (with Bonnie Dee)
Awakening Beauty (with Bonnie Dee)

Demon Lover

Bonnie Dee and Marie Treanor

SAMHAIN
PUBLISHING

Samhain Publishing, Ltd.
577 Mulberry Street, Suite 1520
Macon, GA 31201
www.samhainpublishing.com

Demon Lover

Print ISBN: 978-1-60928-014-7
Digital ISBN: 978-1-60504-979-3

Editing by Linda Ingmanson
Cover by Mandy M. Roth

First Samhain Publishing, Ltd. electronic publication: April 2010
First Samhain Publishing, Ltd. print publication: March 2011

Dedication

For everyone who had difficulty believing in fairytale happiness with a man who marries for greed. Enjoy the real "Rumpelstiltskin"...

Prologue

"Is your name Charles? Oliver? Harold?" Gwyneth's pulse pounded, and she shivered despite the fact she held the precious trump card up her sleeve. Her husband King Midas, the courtiers and soldiers all looked on, frozen as they had been from the moment the devil arrived in a thunderclap and a puff of sulfurous black smoke. Literally frozen by some magic force that thickened the air around them.

"No." The evil being's deep voice reverberated through the room, sending a chill down her spine and making the hair on her nape prickle. As menacing as a towering black thunderhead threaded with crackling lightning, the dark-shrouded figure dominated the throne room of the castle. Gwyneth longed to throw back his hood and behold his face just once.

"Brandon? Sylvester? Archibald? James?"

Why was she playing this dangerous game when her child's very life was at stake? She should simply spit out the horrid name her spy had overheard and win Brea's freedom. A demon from hell couldn't break a deal, could he? Surely he was bound by his word.

"No. Are you prepared to concede, to pay me what you owe?" A cool voice came from the dark depths of the hood.

Gwyneth exhaled slowly, trying to rein in her racing heart. The warmth of victory swelled through her, but she willed herself not to show it with a smug smile. No point in angering her enemy.

"Is your name perhaps"—she paused and licked her lips—"Rumpelstiltskin?"

There was dead silence in the room for the space of three heartbeats. Brea stirred in her cradle and gave a soft gurgle. Gwyneth glanced from the hooded figure to her husband, whose frightened gaze was riveted on the intruder.

Gwyneth knew she was correct. She'd received an eyewitness account of this cloaked demon waltzing around a campfire, gloating over her inability to guess his ridiculous name.

"Is your name Rumpelstiltskin?" she repeated.

The dark being strode forward, stopping only a few paces from her and the cradle.

"No. It is not." He reached for the baby.

For a moment, Queen Gwyneth froze, unable to fathom his answer, then she darted between him and the cradle, intercepting his black-gloved hands as they reached for her precious daughter. She snatched up Brea and clutched the baby to her breast too tightly, making the infant squawk in indignation.

"You lie! I know that's your name. I won't let you take my baby."

"Madam, I never lie, and the child is mine." He moved closer.

Gwyneth caught the familiar scent of smoke and earth that permeated his clothes. The odor should've turned her stomach, made her gut clench in fear, yet it instantly brought back memories of several long, dark, mysterious nights when he'd talked to her and...touched her while she spun straw into gold.

"I won't harm her. I wish to raise her as my own." His

fingers tightened in the baby's blanket.

"Begone, demon! I'll never let you take her." Gwyneth pushed away his hand.

"I would not be accused of separating a child from its mother," he drawled. "You're welcome to come to the underworld with us, lovely Gwyneth. If you dare to give up your wealth and title."

"No!" Midas cried. Maybe he cared for Gwyneth and Brea more than she'd thought. More likely he feared losing the source of his riches—not that she could've spun one golden thread if it weren't for the magical creature who now claimed their child in payment.

"Guards, seize him!" The king yelled quite futilely as everyone in the room, except, apparently, Gwyneth, was still frozen in place.

The black figure loomed over the queen and her child. His cloak seemed to billow in an unseen wind, and the air around them was charged as if from an approaching storm.

Gwyneth clutched Brea and stared into the depths of the hood, trying to glimpse a pair of eyes, trying to make a connection as she begged for mercy, but it was like trying to look down a well. A person might catch a glimmer of water at the bottom, but it was simply too dark to see anything clearly.

"Please, sir, leave my baby alone. I will come with you if that is what you desire, but this poor, innocent child has done nothing. Why should she pay for my unholy bargain?"

"Unholy?" A harsh bark of laughter came from the figure. "You think me some kind of devil? Well, maybe I am, but I'm not the one who was willing to give up her baby in exchange for a pile of gold."

Neither was I. It wasn't my fault. I was trying to save my life. Gwyneth wanted to protest and explain her actions, but excuses would not move him. She gripped his wrist, solid and strong beneath the black gloves—not an incorporeal spirit, but a demon of flesh and blood, as she well knew. She stared into the hood, searching for the face she couldn't see, and made her offer again.

"I will come with you. I will do anything you want. *Anything.*" She emphasized the words with promise in her eyes and imagined she heard a hitch in his breathing. "But please leave Brea out of it."

The creature gave a moment's pause. Gwyneth's heart lifted, rising like a bird in flight. Then another gust of wind blew through the room, swirling around them, and her fleeting hope was dashed, its wings shredded.

"I never break a deal. I will take the child as we agreed. Whether you come with her or not is up to you."

The choice he offered was not a true choice. Of course, she would stay with her baby. "Very well then." She bowed her head. "Let it be done."

"Don't be afraid. It will only last a moment," the midnight-drenched voice whispered. Then the hurricane breeze rose, crackling with energy like lightning. Gwyneth's hair rose on her arms and her head. She held Brea to her breast, feeling her daughter's warm, heavy weight, smelling the milky scent of her breath as the infant cried and wiggled.

Darkness whirled around them. Was it the storm or the demon's cloak encompassing them? Gwyneth couldn't see. Her vision went black and she felt her body lifted. Strong arms wrapped around her, holding her tightly as she was swept away through space. She closed her eyes and screamed inside. She couldn't open her mouth to scream aloud; the pressure of the air was too great. Would it crush Brea's delicate little chest? Oh, God, what had brought her to this? How had she imagined she could escape a deal with the devil himself?

Chapter One

Gwyneth had been scrubbing bird droppings off the floor of the back porch when it began. Such a mundane task to herald the day on which her whole life would change.

Wrens had nested under the eaves, and she was too soft-hearted to drive them away while they had hatchlings. As a result, the birds shat on the porch railings and the floor every time they flew in or out of their nests. Gwyneth couldn't abide the mess and scrubbed the area clean every day, in addition to all her other chores.

She'd kept house for her father, the miller, ever since her mother had died when she was a little girl. Cleaning the house, preparing meals, working in the garden, milking the goats, occasionally taking orders at the mill—these tasks filled her life. She was fairly content, although she dreamed of doing these same duties in a home of her own with a young, handsome husband sitting at her table and sleeping in her bed each night.

But while Gwyneth dreamed of love and home, her father had bigger plans for her—and for himself. He bragged on his daughter's beauty to anyone who would listen, embarrassing her to the depths of her being with his prattling on about her long, golden hair, her sky-blue eyes, her rose-red lips and her smooth, pale skin. Her beauty was his wealth. Richard Miller planned to find a wealthy husband for Gwyneth who would ensure him a comfortable old age.

Word of her loveliness spread across the country. Men came to gape at her as if she were a prize cow nearly ready to be auctioned off.

"You see, she's a hard worker, too. A perfect housewife," her father might boast as he showed her off while she gathered eggs in the hen coop.

He even brought men into the house to observe her sewing in the parlor. "Her hands are as delicate as water lilies. See the tiny stitches she takes with her needle."

Gwyneth dreaded the day he'd escort them into her bedroom to watch her washing up. "See her fine, white body, slender and swaying like a reed," she imagined him saying as the leering men looked on.

But it was while she was on her hands and knees scrubbing a stubborn white dropping from the porch floorboards that her father's boasting reached the zenith of foolishness. It was the day King Midas's steward came to call at the humble miller's house, for word of the man's astonishingly gorgeous daughter had reached the royal ears.

"She's right over here." Gwyneth heard her father's voice before she saw him coming around the corner of the house. "You'll see. She's everything I promised and more. The king himself would be struck dumb with desire by such a beauty."

A man in a peacock blue brocade coat with a red sash across his chest strode alongside her father. He frowned as he picked his way across the yard, avoiding goose crap—birds were the bane of Gwyneth's life—and stopped before he reached the porch.

"Bring the girl out to me. I'm not walking another step in barnyard filth."

Gwyneth set her scrub brush in the bucket of soapy water and rose, wiping her hands on her apron.

The well-dressed man in the yard saw her and his eyes widened. "You tell the truth, Miller. She is every bit as exquisite as the rumors claim."

Gwyneth wanted to run into the house and slam the door behind her. Instead, she came to the porch railing and bobbed a curtsy. "May I bring you something to drink, sir?"

He waved a hand. "No, miss, that won't be necessary. I've seen enough. I'll be on my way." The steward turned on his heel and headed back in the direction from which he'd come.

"Wait! Wait, sir," her father cried, and she cringed inside at the desperation in his tone. "I haven't told you everything. Not only is my daughter an excellent cook, a talented needlewoman, a sublime singer and a remarkable beauty, but she can also, uh, spin straw into gold!" His last words were nearly a shout as he trotted after the retreating back of the king's servant.

The man stopped short. "Excuse me?"

Gwyneth's father hurried toward him, head bobbing. "That's right, spin straw into gold. An amazing talent the likes of which even a king has never seen. Such a talent would surely be worthy of taking a woman to wife. Don't you agree, sir?"

Gwyneth gasped. Her heart stopped beating for a moment, and she clutched a hand to her chest. Her father had gone mad! He would be jailed for his insolence. The mill would be foreclosed on, and perhaps Gwyneth would be thrown into prison for good measure. What was he thinking, making such a preposterous statement?

But the steward turned slowly and stared at her father as if trying to decide whether to hear him out or slap him in the stocks. "Gold, you say? That is an outrageous claim."

"But true."

The man's eyes narrowed. He stroked his full moustache and gazed at Gwyneth, then at the house and yard. "If the girl can truly spin straw into gold, why do you live in this hovel? Show me some of the gold."

"Oh, but you see, sir, the timing must be just right. The full moon... And only once every eighteen years. On the fifth month of the year. That's what the, er, magic woman who blessed her with this gift told us on the day she was born. You see, Gwyneth is a very special girl. Will you introduce her to the king?"

Gwyneth closed her eyes and swallowed hard. *Please, father, stop talking right now before you dig us in any deeper.*

"You already told me the girl is eighteen. This *is* the fifth month of the year, and the full moon takes place over the next three nights," the king's advisor pointed out. "If she can truly do all you say, I'll take her to the castle this very afternoon and test her tonight to see if she's worthy of being wedded to the king."

Father stood with his back to her, but she could almost hear him swallow as he was caught in his lie. Gwyneth's heart plummeted still farther, landing in her shoe. If he had to claim something so crazy, couldn't he at least have made it impossible to prove?

The steward strode toward the porch, ignoring any goose droppings he might flatten under his polished boots. He stared at Gwyneth. "Is it true, miss? Can you spin straw into gold?"

"I don't know, sir," she answered truthfully, trying not to expose her father's lie or add to it. "I've never tried to before."

He snapped his fingers and beckoned her as if she was a dog. "Come along. I'm taking you to the king. He can decide for himself if he wishes to put you to the test. Likely it's all nonsense, but one never knows with these things, and it wouldn't do to miss out on an opportunity for His Majesty. It might be my head that would roll."

Gwyneth began to untie her apron. "I should change. I'm not dressed for an audience with the king." Anything to stall for time. Maybe she and her father could sneak out of the back of the house and run away.

"Doesn't matter." The man snapped his fingers again. "Come along, girl."

She hurried down the steps and across the yard to him. Around the corner of the house, she beheld a gorgeous carriage parked in the front drive between the house and the slowly turning wheel of the gristmill. The gilded royal insignia decorated the door of the carriage.

Her heart must have risen from her shoe, because it dove back down again as a new jolt of terror ripped through her. She should end this now, tell the man it was all a foolish mistake. Would they punish Father and leave her out of it? Could she do that to him? He was her father, after all, no matter how much she despised his behavior sometimes. What if the penalty was worse than the stocks or jail time? Could a commoner be beheaded for inventing such a lie?

Silence seemed to be her only option. Gwyneth felt as if her lips were sewn shut so she couldn't possibly deny her father's claim. She rode in the fancy carriage toward her destiny, so sick with fear she was afraid if she opened her mouth she might vomit on the purple velvet upholstery.

When the carriage reached the palace and she was ushered from it, Gwyneth was bombarded by a barrage of images: a flagstone courtyard; mammoth, ornate doors; an imposing front hallway filled with armor and paintings. She was left to wait on a large gilt chair in a parlor which could have encompassed her entire house.

After nearly an hour, the steward returned. "Before you can meet the king, you must be appropriately attired."

He summoned maidservants who took her to a

bedchamber, dressed her in a sumptuous, pale green silk gown and embroidered slippers. They arranged her hair, rouged her cheeks, draped her in jewels, then returned her to the steward so he could escort her to the king's private chamber.

"When you enter the room, keep your head bowed. Don't address the king until he speaks to you, or approach him until he tells you to come forward. Be certain to drop a deep curtsy and don't raise your eyes to meet his. Can you remember all that, girl?"

"Yes, sir." She caught her breath as servants opened the tall, highly polished door and the steward seized her elbow and propelled her forward. All she could see was her own shoes, the colorful tapestry of the carpet beneath them and a flash of the steward's boots as he walked alongside her.

He squeezed her elbow, and she stopped walking and waited, dying to look up and see the king. She listened to the soft pad of royal footsteps on the rich carpet as he walked toward her and stopped in front of her. Should she curtsy now or wait for him to acknowledge her first? She couldn't remember.

A white-gloved hand reached out, took hold of her chin and tilted her face. Pale gray eyes looked down a long, narrow-bridged nose into her eyes. "My Lord, she really is a beauty, isn't she? But about this other thing, do you really believe it, Wallace?"

"I don't know, Your Majesty. It sounds highly suspect, but there's no harm in testing her."

"Quite true." The king released her chin and stepped back. She risked another glance, taking in his high forehead, fair hair pulled back into a neat queue, his long, angular face, the jewel encrusted lapels of his jacket—a trifle showy, but then a king could wear what he liked.

Gwyneth took the opportunity to curtsy.

"You're a very lovely girl, Gwyneth," King Midas addressed her at last. "I certainly hope your father's telling the truth about this fairy blessing or whatever it is because I should sorely hate to cleave that pretty yellow head from that creamy white neck. It would be rather like decapitating a buttercup. Flowers were made to be enjoyed, not destroyed, and you are a rare and exquisite blossom, which I should enjoy inhaling deeply in the future."

She had no idea how to reply. A threat, a compliment and a suggestive comment all combined? There was no response she could give, and so she remained silent.

"Is there anything you'd like to say, Buttercup?" the king continued. "A confession, perhaps, or maybe just a salutation."

Good God, was he giving her a chance to make an excuse and win her freedom? Should she tell him everything right now and beg for her father's life and her own? But what if it was a trick and he had them executed anyway? If she could prolong this situation until the end of tonight, perhaps her father, at least, would have a chance to make an escape.

"I'm deeply honored to meet you, Your Highness." She could barely speak above a whisper. She cleared her throat and tried again. "As for the claims about my beauty or my abilities, I cannot speak to either topic without appearing vain or proud. It is for others to say whether they find me beautiful, and for time to tell whether I can perform up to expectations."

There. That would have to do. Neither an admission of guilt nor a claim to have abilities she didn't possess.

"I shall look forward to talking with you more, little Buttercup." The handsome king smiled as if he'd never mentioned possibly killing her. "For now, you shall be given dinner while a room full of straw is prepared for you."

Straw. Gwyneth swallowed the bile that rose in her throat. She'd never have imagined that simple word could strike terror in her heart. She curtsied again before backing out of the room and away from the king's presence.

When the door had closed behind her, the steward seized her arm once more and propelled her along the hallway. He took her to a formal dining room where a single place setting graced one end of a long table.

After she was seated, a series of servants with silver dishes offered her delicacies which she refused despite the rumbling of her stomach. She was too anxious to choke down food.

"You really should eat something," the steward said. "This may be your last meal."

Gwyneth glanced up sharply. He must know her father's story was a lie. Perhaps both he and the king were having a joke at her expense. It would explain their sly words and arch tones. They were merely making a game for themselves. Playing with her like a cat played with a mouse before killing it.

She straightened her shoulders and firmed her chin. "I'm ready now. Take me to the room and we'll find out if I can perform the task you've set for me."

Gwyneth managed to keep up her brave front as he marched her along the hallway and down a flight of stairs to a subterranean series of chambers. She showed no expression as a soldier opened the door and escorted her into a room so full of straw the dust floating in the air choked her and made her sneeze. She bit her trembling lower lip and kept her face still as she regarded a large spinning wheel standing in the center of bales of straw, and she shed not a tear as she faced Steward Wallace one last time.

"Good luck, my girl. I fear you're going to need it." He smiled at her with perhaps a touch of sympathy before walking from the room.

The door slammed shut behind him. There was a clang of

metal on metal as the bolts shot home. She was locked into a windowless room with no hope of escape.

Gwyneth walked over to the spinning wheel, touched the sharp point of the spindle, then set the empty wheel turning. The wooden axle creaked as the wheel spun around. She wandered over to one of the piles of loose straw, conveniently pulled from a bound bale for her use, and picked up a handful.

The stiff yellow stalks sifted through her fingers and fell to the floor. Her father was such a fool. If a person were to spin any grass into golden thread, it should be hay, not straw. Hay was much more pliable.

The ridiculous thought seized hold of her, and she began to laugh. She pressed her hands over her mouth to hold back her laughter, but it burst through. She laughed and laughed until tears ran down her cheeks. Then she sank onto the little stool facing the spinning wheel and sobbed until her breath hitched in her chest.

Oh, God, please, God, I haven't asked you for anything since the night my mother died. You couldn't spare her then. But will you spare me now? Please, help me. Do something to save me. Send me a miracle.

There was no miracle. Why would there be? Why would God vindicate her father's barefaced lie? It wasn't as if he'd made his ridiculous claim through any motive purer than plain greed.

Gwyneth wiped her eyes on her borrowed sleeve and straightened. It wasn't her nature to give in, and now that she'd wept out her tension and despair at the impossibility of her task, she decided to give it a go.

She stood and dragged a bound bale of straw closer to the wheel and sat to begin. She ignored the horrible noise the spinning wheel made and tried to concentrate. She tried to wish magic into her tingling fingers, gold into the dull, dead straw.

She tried praying while she spun. But no determination in the world could accomplish the impossible and, as time wore on, despair began to rise once more.

She had no idea of the time. She seemed to have been there for hours, futilely spinning straw into thinner strands of straw by the light of the single lantern. Her hands hurt, her back ached and she imagined the sun rising in the sky. The last sunrise of her life, and she wouldn't even see it.

Tears prickled her eyelids. As panic began to rise once more, she got up and ran to the door, testing the security of the bolts. Surely there was a way out of here. Why had she not just admitted to the king that she couldn't do this? So what if they'd killed her? At least she'd have been spared this night of awful anticipation.

The door wouldn't budge, even when she pounded it with her fists and threw her entire body against it. Leaving it, she felt her way around all four solid walls. No hint of a hidden door met her questing hands. In desperation, she began to move the straw around the room in order to scrutinize every inch of the stone floor.

There was no escape. She'd always known it, just as she'd always known there was no earthly chance of spinning straw into gold.

"I always took my life for granted," she whispered aloud, sinking into the useless straw. "I never realized how much I wanted it… Not just my silly dreams of a beautiful future with some wonderful husband, but even the everyday drudgery. I'd give *anything*, just to have life."

She closed her eyes as the silent tears poured down her cheeks, giving in at last to total despair, total loss.

A loud crash like thunder exploded through the sealed room. Gwyneth jumped, her eyes snapping open. Smoke billowed around her, emitting some powerful, sulfurous stench.

Astonished, she gazed into it, and after an instant made out the tall, cowled figure of a man.

He stood perfectly still, the cowl pointing toward her. His voice seemed to echo, as if from some deep cavern. “Did you say *anything*?”

Chapter Two

Curiously, Gwyneth felt no real fear, perhaps because she was too stunned, perhaps because she'd already sunk so low. Somewhere, she realized she should be very frightened, that danger of kinds she couldn't even imagine surrounded the black hooded figure emerging from the smoke.

But mostly, she was aware of relief. "There *is* a way out!" she exclaimed.

"There is always a way out," her visitor answered. His voice was deep, low, almost sepulchral, sending shivers down her spine. "It is just a matter of finding it. And being prepared to take it."

He moved through the smoke and bent toward her, stretching down his hand. It, too, was black, encased in a long gauntlet. Dazed, Gwyneth took his fingers before she meant to and was drawn to her feet. He smelled of rich earth and smoke. His hand seemed to engulf hers, burning her skin even through the thickness of his glove. And yet the effect was not unpleasant. Perhaps because he'd given her hope.

She peered into the darkness of his cowl. Somewhere in its depths, two eyes glittered, but she could make out nothing more. He stood still and silent, not yet releasing her hand. She had the feeling she was being assessed. Well, no one had ever complained about her looks.

She drew in her breath. "I'll take it," she said fervently. "If you would be so good as to show me the way."

He released her hand, turning his head to look around the straw-filled room. "What exactly is your problem?" he inquired.

"I'm locked in. I can't get out. And in the morning, the king will execute me."

The cowl returned to face her. "Does he think you're some kind of animal, to surround you with bales of straw?"

A breath of laughter escaped Gwyneth, just when she thought she'd never laugh again. "Believe it or not, I'm supposed to spin this straw into gold. If I can't—and obviously I can't!—I am to die."

"So you want a way out. And would do anything for life."

"It will be a difficult life," she acknowledged. "I'll have to run away, go into hiding with nothing, perhaps try to escape to another country, but I'm a hard worker and will soon pay my way."

"A hard worker," he repeated, and she thought he was studying her borrowed dress and jewels. Once more, he reached out and took her hand, turning up the rough palm and fingers. Ashamed, she tugged it free. "You are a woman of contradictions. Fortunately, you intrigue me."

"Then you'll show me the way out?" Gwyneth said eagerly.

"I'll show you *a* way out, if you wish it. But you must be aware, there is always a price."

I'd give anything...

She swallowed. "I'd give you this necklace, these rings, but the jewelry isn't mine. It belongs to the king."

"I don't want his jewels."

"Then what will you take?"

The cowl moved. Two gleaming eyes held her gaze. She

thought she could see a flash of teeth, the movement of lips. "For turning all this straw into gold that you might go free and return to your life?"

Gwyneth's mouth fell open. "You can't do that. No one can. It was just a silly, ill-conceived boast of my father's!"

"But if I could, would you want it?"

"Is that my only way out? To perpetuate the lie?"

"Can you think of another?"

"I could escape the way you came in."

"Where I go, you would not wish to follow."

"I'm tough," she pointed out eagerly. "And spry."

He seemed to be considering her desire to go with him, then suddenly shook his head. "I would not take you under these circumstances. Besides, is the life of a fugitive so attractive?"

"No," she admitted, longing with unexpected strength to scrub some more wren droppings off her father's porch. She smiled a little tentatively. "The truth is, I doubt your ability to spin straw into gold. I don't see how it can be done."

"I'll show you. For..." The whiteness of teeth gleamed again. "For a kiss."

She blinked. "A kiss?"

"A kiss."

"But I don't know you," she blurted.

His breath came out in a rush. He might have been laughing. "I suspect that by the time you've spun all this straw into gold, you'll imagine you know me well enough to give me your lips for a few moments. Is it a huge price to pay for your life?"

"N-no," she admitted.

"Then what's the matter? Haven't you been kissed before?"

"No," she said again. "I slapped the last boy who tried."

"Well, you can slap me, too, if you want, but I will insist on the kiss."

Gwyneth became aware that the butterflies in her stomach were far from unpleasant. She admitted to curiosity, about kisses in general and this mysterious stranger's in particular. However, though she may have been innocent in practice, she was far from naive in theory.

"*Just* a kiss?" she demanded.

The cowl moved, as if he was silently laughing at her again. "I won't ravish you, if that's what you mean. I ask for a kiss, and that is exactly what I will take. On your lips," he added, as though to quell any further doubts.

Gwyneth's body began to flush. She'd never imagined he meant anything else, but now that the idea was in her mind, it ran riot. Kisses on her throat and shoulders, on her breasts, which had begun to ache inexplicably.

"Well?" her visitor prompted.

She blinked to dispel the unwanted images in her mind, and took a deep breath. "Yes, please," she said.

"Good." He swung away from her. "Then collect a good armful of straw and sit at your wheel. You have a lot of spinning to do."

"Sir, I've already tried," she protested, disappointed at this pointless instruction.

He sighed, and Gwyneth caught a more powerful whiff of his peculiar, smoky scent. "You have nothing to lose," he reminded her. "Not even a kiss. Unless the straw becomes gold."

Whenever he said the word "kiss", something seemed to jump in her stomach. It was too unfamiliar to be recognized, but she thought it might actually have been excitement. How could a kiss excite her when her life still hung in the balance?

So, obediently, she went and picked up an armful of straw and sat at the wheel.

"Begin," her visitor commanded. "Don't be too dainty. We haven't got much time."

"Is it dawn?" she asked, alarmed.

"Not yet. Begin."

This time, the wheel didn't grind and protest. It ate up the straw like wool. And before her eyes it spun into a thin filament of gold. Stunned, she stopped and touched it. Cold and hard. Her lips parted. Her eyes turned up to the cowled figure who stood at her shoulder.

For the first time since he'd appeared, rationality began to poke at her stunned, exhausted brain. There was no way into this room. She couldn't leave with him. Unless she'd fallen asleep and was dreaming, he'd given her the impossible ability to turn straw into gold at a spinning wheel.

"Who are you?" she whispered. *What are you?* Politeness prevented the second question from forming, but he answered neither. Merely, his lips moved inside the cowl, tempting her with the desire to see them, to see all of his face instead of tantalizing glimpses of tiny shadowed parts of it.

"Continue," he said.

She sat among a growing pile of golden thread. The wheel spun as she shoved handfuls of straw through, faster and faster. It seemed no finesse was necessary. It just had to go through the motions of being spun, because that was what she'd promised to do. The strange man who made it happen merely watched her from a few feet away, where he sat on one of the remaining piles of straw. Mostly, he didn't speak. Nor did he trouble to move the straw for her. As if it had to be all *her* work. Apart from the magic, of course. The funny thing was, his silent presence soothed her. Perhaps it was just comparison with the terrible loneliness and despair of her first few hours in this room.

And then he spoke. "What is your name?" His deep, dark voice startled her so that she lost the rhythm of her spinning and turned toward him with a jerk.

"Gwyneth," she said breathlessly as she pushed a pile of straw toward the wheel. Apart from where he sat, this was the last bundle. If she wasn't dreaming.

"Gwyneth," he repeated, as if savoring the word on his tongue. He seemed to like it. Her skirts brushed against his legs as she shoved the straw across the floor. He had good legs, she noted inanely. Long, with muscled thighs inside their black, silky casing. He wore black, shining boots that stretched over his knees. "Gwyneth, why do you wear the king's jewels?"

"They dressed me like a doll to meet him."

"Why?" he asked again.

She flopped back onto the stool and seized a handful of straw. Her other hand was already spinning the wheel. "I suppose because he doesn't like to sully his audience chamber with ugliness."

"Are you ugly without jewels?"

"I don't *think* so. But my dress—my own dress—is ugly."

"You are not a lady of the court."

Borrowed clothes and jewels didn't make her a lady. They never would. She gave a twisted little smile. "How could you tell?"

"I observe. Over the years, I've watched, and even talked with, several. You are different."

"How?" she asked curiously. "My accent? My hands? My manners?"

"Yes."

Stupid to feel deflated. She stuffed more straw in and spun it wildly.

"Partly," he added. He no longer sounded quite so certain, causing her to spare a glance at the hidden face. "Your manners are better than theirs. And you are educated."

She made a face. "My father made sure of it. He thinks a rich man will marry me."

"Do you?"

"It doesn't seem really important right now," she said, almost surprised. She smiled. "I suppose facing death alters your priorities. I wanted a home of my own, a wonderful, handsome husband, a child to love. And I wouldn't have objected to pretty dresses and jewels. Who would?"

"So your family is poor? And your father hoped to make money from you?"

She flushed. "It wasn't like that." *Was it?*

"And what will you do now that you've performed the king's task?"

I have! I really have! Almost...

Euphoria made her smile brilliantly at the black cloaked figure. "I'll kiss you, of course." As soon as the words were out, she regretted them, flushing hotly as she added, "And go home to my father, hopefully to stop him talking any more nonsense."

She pushed the cobweb tangle of gold away from her and scraped up the last of her pile of straw.

"And," she added, watching the fibers spin into another delicate golden spiral, "I will think of you every day with gratitude. Thank you for your kindness to me."

He didn't respond to that. She didn't mind. It was something she had to say, and it came from her heart. The kiss was his price and she'd pay it gladly with as much excitement as fear. But the words and the fervent feeling behind them she gave freely.

Gwyneth stood once more and walked toward him. She had the impression his eyes followed her, though she couldn't see them. As she drew closer, his head lifted. She was sure she glimpsed his lips, the lips that would kiss hers, slightly parted in the shadows of the cowl.

She swallowed, trying to still the gamboling butterflies in her stomach. "Excuse me," she said. "This is the last straw."

He stood at once, and she realized all over again his height and presence. He was too close to her, blocking her access to the straw behind him. His distinctive rich, earthy scent, just tinged with smoke, assailed her nostrils, filling her mind with unanswered questions as well as a longing to see his face. He would have to take down the hood to kiss her.

Shockingly, her pussy clenched, reminding her of vague, hot dreams and unfulfilled desires. Perhaps when he kissed her, he would touch her body... But he had promised not to, and never in a million years would she admit that she wanted his touch most in that moist, tender place between her thighs.

"I am not kind." His abrupt words broke into her wayward thoughts, distracting her—thank God!—and making her smile.

"Of course you are," she said warmly, and he, apparently struck dumb, stood aside to let her gather and push the straw across to the wheel.

As she spun, she was very aware of him walking toward her. He moved lightly, his boots making no sound on the rough stone floor, and with strange, swift grace. His enveloping cloak swung around his big, mysterious body, but his cowl never stirred.

His presence at her side unnerved her as his more distant companionship had not. To cover it, she rushed into speech.

"What of you?" she demanded, a little too forcefully. "What is your name?"

"You couldn't pronounce it."

"I could try. Where are you from?"

"You wouldn't believe me."

"Tonight, I'd believe anything." Reaching for some more straw at his feet, she cast him a quick glance. His eyes glinted inside the hood. "How *did* you get in here?"

He lifted one disparaging hand. "You would call it magic."

"What would you call it?"

"Life." He might have been smiling. He sounded as if he was. Encouraged, she smiled back.

"Are you an angel?"

This time, she felt the breath of definite laughter stirring the hair on the top of her head. "Not that. I'm more likely to be a demon. Have you finished?"

She stared at the empty floor, clenched her stiff hands, the fingers cut and bloodied from handling the rough straw. "Yes," she whispered, and gazed up at him in wonder. "Yes, I have. I've done it. You've saved my life."

He held out his hand in silent command. When she laid her own in it, she saw that her fingers trembled, perhaps in relief, perhaps in fear. She rose to her feet.

"Then let me take my price."

Something jolted in her stomach, spread wickedly lower. She nodded.

His hand slid up her wrist to her left shoulder. His free hand tipped up her chin. She felt the coolness of his leather glove against her heated flesh.

"Close your eyes," he whispered.

She did, though determined to open them later on and see

him. The soft fabric of his hood brushed her face—was he still wearing it after all? His breath stirred her cheek, her lips, and then he touched her mouth.

His lips were warm, unexpectedly soft, caressing hers until they parted and then sank on her mouth. The butterflies in her stomach seemed to catch fire. Flame licked down between her thighs, and yet apart from the light pressure of his gloved hands on her shoulder and chin, he only touched her mouth.

She liked to be kissed. Gladness flooded her. She relaxed, letting her lips part under his, and his mouth sank deeper, opening hers further. She gave a tiny gasp as his tongue dipped between her teeth, as if he were tasting her. The flames below began to burn.

Her savior explored her mouth with gentle, aching care. His tongue flickered around hers as if inviting it to dance, and daringly, she let hers slide along his in a caress that aroused even greater pleasure.

Gwyneth was lost in her first kiss.

When he released her mouth, she couldn't suppress her mewl of disappointment. She remembered her eyes were still closed after all, and snapped them open. Twin points of light gleamed at her as he drew back. His face was all darkness and shadows because he still wore the cowl. It didn't seem important. What mattered now was that he no longer kissed her, and she wanted him to quite desperately.

Reaching up, she slid her hand inside the hood and touched the skin of his face, warm and a little rough from the stubble on his jaw. His breath seemed to hitch and then still. She wanted to speak, to ask for another kiss, but couldn't find the words. Instead, mutely, she lifted her face inside the cowl, seeing only tempting shadows and hooded eyes, until she found his lips with hers and sighed with pleasure.

For an instant, his were perfectly still. As though she'd

stunned him. And then it all changed. One arm swept her hard against his body, and she gasped into his mouth as it bore down on hers. Everything about him was hard now, his purposeful, demanding lips, his chest against her crushed, pebbled nipples, his muscular thighs against her hips, his cock straining against her abdomen.

Excitement soared. Especially when his hand swept down her back over the swell of her buttocks, pulling her even closer to his cock. She could feel its outline growing against her and wanted more. His questing hand slid up her body, over her hip and waist and the side of her breast. Pangs of delight twisted through her. Moaning, she moved against him to allow him access, and his palm closed over her breast.

Sweetness suffused her body. Without meaning to, she pushed into his hand and felt his gloved thumb caress back and forth over her hard, pleading nipple.

As suddenly as it had begun, it was over. His hands on her shoulders held her away from him. Her swollen lips felt cold. Her whole body trembled with reaction, although it was some comfort to hear the swiftness of his breath. And yet she still couldn't see his face.

He said, "You paid more than my price."

"I wasn't paying." She didn't know what she was saying. Half-ashamed at her wantonness, she still wanted more.

"I have a feeling we'll meet again."

"How will I know you if I can't see your face?"

"It won't matter. I know you." His hand lifted off her shoulder. One gloved finger touched her lips and slid away. "By your kiss."

He stepped back several paces. A clap of thunder sounded, and the familiar belch of smoke she remembered from his arrival filled the room. When it cleared, he had vanished.

Chapter Three

The door opened before the smoke had completely cleared, and Gwyneth whirled to face the guard and the steward, Wallace. Both men entered the room, identical expressions of shock blooming on their faces as they beheld the tangled masses of golden thread that spilled in shimmering profusion near the spinning wheel.

"I didn't have time to roll skeins, and you didn't provide me with spools," Gwyneth coolly apologized. She couldn't help the smug satisfaction that nestled warmly in her heart at the sight of their wide eyes and gaping mouths.

"Request His Majesty's presence here," Wallace ordered the guard. "Hurry!"

Gwyneth pressed her fingers to her lower back and stretched the kinks from it. Now that her mysterious visitor was gone and her life saved, she realized the toll last night's work had taken on her. Her fingers and palms were raw, and her back ached terribly from carrying bundles and stooping over the spinning wheel.

"How...How did you do this?" the man stammered as he went to one of the piles and fingered a fine gold filament.

She stifled a yawn. "I don't know. It's a talent that comes from beyond me."

Would the king dismiss her now that she'd performed the

task? When she saw her father again, she would berate him for his dangerous bragging, which had almost gotten them both killed. For too long, she'd kept silent, an obedient and well-mannered daughter. Now it was time to speak her mind to him, about this, about all of his bragging and how it made her feel like a pretty object.

"Your father spoke the truth. I can't believe it," the steward continued to marvel as he lifted a hank of gold and weighed it in his hand. "The king will be well-pleased with you and with me for bringing you to him."

His voice seemed to come from far away. Gwyneth's head felt fuzzy, she was so exhausted from her sleepless night and from the mind-numbing terror of believing her life was near its end. She wanted nothing more than to curl up on the floor and sleep...after a visit to the privy, for her bladder was near bursting from hours in captivity.

"Will I be allowed to go home now?" she asked Wallace.

"That will be for His Majesty to decide, but I shouldn't imagine he'll let a prize like you slip through his fingers."

Instantly, her drowsiness vanished and her nerves jangled. Surely the king wouldn't expect her to repeat her performance. What if he did? Would the dark stranger help her again or would she be left alone to face the penalty she'd escaped the first time?

Minutes ticked past as they waited for the king. Gwyneth's gaze roamed over the piles of gold which glinted faintly in the lantern's glow. The enormity of the astonishing, miraculous thing she'd done crashed over her. Who was the hooded man? An angel as she'd called him, or a demon as he claimed? A being which possessed such powerful magic was certainly more than human. Her lips tingled as she remembered his kiss and the greedy, wanton way she'd begged for more. Perhaps that had been magic, too. A spell he'd cast over her to make her want him.

Her musings and the awkward silence between her and the steward ended as booted footsteps echoed down the hallway. Moments later, King Midas himself appeared in the doorway. His handsome face twisted in an equally comic look of surprise, his brows shooting up and his mouth dropping open. He didn't say a word as he entered the room and walked slowly around, gazing at the piles of gold.

Gwyneth waited, throbbing fingers clenched lightly at her sides, and at last he turned to her. He clapped, applauding her in an exaggerated manner. "Brava, Buttercup. You're truly a marvel, as beauteous as the day is long and a magician to boot."

He extended a hand to her, and Gwyneth reluctantly offered hers. The king bent and kissed the back of her fingers, then clasped them between his. His palms were cool and dry and somehow reminded her of snake skin. She wanted to pull away.

"You have earned a rest and pampering fit for a princess. I shall meet you later in the day for dinner and we will talk further. For now, please go with Wallace, who will show you to a bed chamber and provide for all your needs." At last he released her hand. She dropped it back to her side.

"I appreciate your gracious offer, Your Highness, but my father needs me at home. Will you now allow me to return to him?"

"We can discuss all that over dinner." He evaded her question and waved for Wallace to accompany Gwyneth from her gold-filled prison.

He took her to a bed chamber where she was met by a fleet of maidservants. She was undressed, bathed, clothed in a night shift and put to bed like a helpless child. Gwyneth would have protested if she wasn't so exhausted, but it felt rather comforting to surrender her body into the care of others. She'd never known such luxury as the ornate, velvet-draped bed where she was to sleep. She sank deep into the goose-down mattress, and the ladies-in-waiting left her alone at last. Before the door closed behind them, she noted a guard standing in the corridor outside. She was still a prisoner, a wren in a gilded cage.

As tired as she was, sleep eluded her for a while. She replayed the past day and night: her father's boasts, her terror at the task set before her and, of course, every second spent with the mysterious man in black. How had he appeared in the room? What was the extent of his power? Could he come to her here if she summoned him?

The last idea filled her with a thrill of excitement as she imagined him looming at the side of her lavish bed, studying her body in the thin nightdress. Touching her. Sliding a hand up her leg beneath the gown. Gwyneth caught her breath. Her inner thighs burned as if they were truly being stroked, and the junction of her thighs was afire. She clamped her legs together in an attempt to soothe the ache, but an assault of images filled her mind and stoked the fire.

She pictured the dark-garbed man climbing onto the bed with her, climbing on top of her and doing all sorts of arousing things with his gloved hands, although she wasn't quite certain what exactly those things might be. She didn't imagine his face or body uncovered. Part of the thrill of her fantasy was in his mysterious, dangerous nature. He had helped her, yes, but she felt quite certain that he was not "good", not in the traditional way the term was defined.

Mostly her fantasy centered on kissing...and kissing...and kissing. The pressure of his mouth on hers, the sinuous slide of his tongue, his powerful hands cradling the base of her head and her back, all of these elements she'd actually experienced and could imagine. He'd also slid his hand up her front to cup her breast. Gwyneth imitated his action and felt the turgid nipple and soft fullness of her breast. Right there, just like that, he'd touched her.

She gathered the fabric of the shift and reached beneath to curve her hand over her mons, the weight of her palm settling warmly. She teased a finger between her folds and felt the wetness there coating it. Slicking her finger through the juices, she brought it higher and tickled the tiny nub where her pleasure lay coiled. What would it feel like to have a cool, gloved hand touch her there?

Gwyneth moaned and lifted her hips, thrusting against her palm as she plucked at her nipple through the nightgown. Her own circling touch on her clitoris and the fantasy of a demon lover abruptly sent a bolt of ecstasy shooting through her. Sparks showered like a bonfire when a piece of damp wood was added.

She groaned and her body arched off the bed, her mind soaring. But when she came down from the peak of bliss, discontent filled her almost immediately. She wanted more, so much more than self-pleasuring. Tired of being a maiden, Gwyneth was ready to know everything about becoming a woman, and she wanted to learn it from the right man. That would *not* be a magical being or a nighttime fantasy, but a real, flesh and blood husband she could build a life with.

With her sexual tension eased, the tension that came from not knowing what the king had in mind for her moved to the forefront of her thoughts. She guessed her value to him had increased from the moment he beheld the piles of spun gold, but what impossible task would he demand of her next? Her situation was still very precarious.

Anxious thoughts turned into anxious dreams as Gwyneth finally slept.

She awakened with a start to a hand shaking her shoulder. The ladies were back for another round of dressing and primping. They combed and coiled her hair, draped her in emeralds, shod her in satin slippers and stood her in front of a long looking glass to behold her new glory. She looked like royalty, but she didn't look like herself.

Nor did she feel like herself as she was ushered down several corridors and flights of stairs to the dining room where the king awaited her. Gwyneth floated apart from her body, watching this stranger make an appropriate deep curtsy to His Majesty before taking her seat at the table.

"You are exquisite, my darling. One might say 'queenly' in your grace and bearing," King Midas complimented her.

Gwyneth inclined her head in acknowledgement. "Thank you, sire. You are too kind." Now would he be kind enough to let her go?

"I hope you rested well and that the ladies assigned to you were satisfactory."

"Yes, sire." She picked up her spoon, and it slipped in the silken glove encasing her fingers. One of the ladies-in-waiting had insisted she wear the gloves to cover her rough hands. Carefully, she scooped a spoonful of soup and swallowed it.

She glanced at the king, and he gazed at her with an expression that reminded her of the cats sitting on the porch watching the nesting wrens. Suddenly, her throat was tight and she doubted she could swallow another bite of the meal, despite the fact that she was starving.

"Gwyneth." It was the first time he'd referred to her by name. "You are a very beautiful and talented woman, despite the fact you are not of noble birth. I will admit I'm intrigued by the fact you can spin straw into gold, but I'm also entranced by your appearance and your manners."

"Thank you, sire." She wasn't certain what response he was looking for, but that seemed a safe one.

"I believe I will make you my wife."

Her throat constricted and her stomach lurched. This was her father's dream come true. It should have been hers as well. Any woman in the land would be thrilled to hear those words coming from the lips of a monarch. So why did she feel sick?

Ignoring her lack of response, Midas went on. "But before I make such a momentous decision as choosing you for the mother of my heirs, I must be absolutely certain you are truly worthy of that honor." He leaned forward, fixing her with his gaze. "Therefore, I have commanded another room full of straw be prepared for you. I would like another demonstration of your inestimable powers."

"Oh, Your Majesty," she whispered and could say no more. Hopefully he'd think she was struck dumb by the honor of being offered his hand in marriage.

He smiled, his white teeth gleaming in the candlelight. "And this time I've provided many spindles to keep the gold thread from tangling."

Chapter Four

Once more Gwyneth waited in the room full of straw, desperate and alone, but with a sliver of hope which she hadn't possessed the previous night. For now she knew there was someone who could give her the magic to perform the impossible task. But what could she do to summon him?

She stood in the center of the room, sneezing as the chaff in the air tickled her nose, and examined the chamber from corner to corner. How *had* he entered the room? Did one of the great stone blocks which made up the walls and floor move aside to provide him entrance? And where exactly had he come from?

She licked her lips and cleared her throat. "Sir," she called softly, "I beseech you to come to me again. I need your help. Please."

There was no answer. The dead silence was disturbed only by a tiny rustle, perhaps of a mouse brought in with one of the bales of straw.

Gwyneth clasped her hands together. "I cannot do this alone. I need your magic. Please, I'll do anything you require if only you will save me once more."

More silence. What if he didn't come this time? Now that the king was convinced she could perform the task, he might take her refusal to accomplish it a second time as willful disobedience—perhaps treason. Could she convince him that her magic power was used up since the full moon of the fifth month was waning? She couldn't be expected to produce gold again until another eighteen years had passed, according to her father's bizarre claim.

She squeezed her eyes shut and tears slipped from the corners to trickle down her cheeks. "Please, I need you," she whispered.

"Then you shall have me, my lady." The voice murmuring near her ear, hot breath tickling her neck, nearly jolted her out of her skin. She started to whirl to face him and her shoulder slammed into his hard chest. He stood right behind her, as solid and immovable as a wall.

One gloved finger reached out and caught the tear which had dripped nearly to her jaw. "Diamonds," he murmured. "More beautiful than the green glass you wear around your neck."

Gwyneth automatically reached up to touch the elaborate emerald necklace that draped her throat. "You're here," was all she could manage to say.

He dipped his hooded head slightly. "Your wish is my command, but as before, I will demand a payment."

What this time? Her heart pounded as she remembered the ravishing kiss last night, the way it had stolen her breath away and made her skin burn.

"I have this necklace." She fingered the cold, hard gems. "Although I don't know how I would explain its loss to the king."

"Then you don't really *have* the necklace if it doesn't belong to you." He stroked a hand down her arm from shoulder to wrist, and her flesh tingled. "But you have other jewels more precious than those. Rubies." He touched her lips lightly with a fingertip. "Star sapphires." He indicated her blue eyes. "And a single precious pearl."

One gloved hand slid down the front of her gown to cup her mound through the layers of silk and petticoats. He pressed hard with his finger on the very bud she had massaged earlier, and warmth bloomed from the sensitive spot.

Gwyneth drew in a sharp breath.

For a sizzling moment they remained locked together with his hand on her pussy the only point of contact, and then, abruptly, the demon stepped away from her. She felt the absence of his commanding presence which had made the air around her positively crackle with energy.

She licked her lips before she spoke. "What would you have me give?"

He looked around the room. "There's more work to be done tonight."

It was true. The room was filled with nearly half as much straw as the previous night.

"I would need more than a kiss this time."

Scissors of fear and excitement snipped through her mask of calm. "How much more?"

"I want to touch you. Everywhere. And I want you to touch me."

Her excitement mounted. He would unmask, then. She would see his face at last. But then the other half of what he demanded struck her. He wanted to see and touch her body—naked. She'd never been naked in front of anyone in her entire life.

At her hesitation, he added, "I will not have sex with you, nor will I force you to do anything you don't enjoy. But I must have something for my trouble."

Gwyneth had no other options, and a deep-seated part of

her wanted to know his touch and to have his gaze travel over her body. Just thinking about it set her afire all over again.

"Very well. It's a deal."

"Then you may begin to spin. I suggest you hurry, as there's a great deal of work to be done and I demand some time at the end of the evening for myself."

Gwyneth gazed at the mountainous bales of straw and empty spindles waiting to be filled. Her fingers were already swollen and sore despite the balm one of the serving women had treated them with. The task before her seemed monumental—*but at least not impossible now*, she reminded herself as she cut the twine on the first bale of straw.

She sat on the stool and fed the strands into the flyer while her foot pumped the treadle, making the wheel spin round. Gold thread began to coil around the first empty bobbin. She fed her lapful of straw into the machine and reached for more, all the while rhythmically pumping her foot up and down. It was impossible to see at what point the strands of straw became metallic gold. The wheel was a blur, the distaff spun and Gwyneth gave up trying to see the moment of change, accepting the magic as she did the mysterious wizard himself.

She hummed softly and rocked in time to the rhythm of her foot on the treadle. All the while she was acutely aware of the man who watched her.

"Do you enjoy spinning?" he suddenly asked.

"When I'm not doing it to save my life, yes."

"What is that song you hum?"

"An old spinning song one of the women in the village taught me. It helps me keep a rhythm so the thread is spun evenly."

"Your mother didn't teach you?"

"No. She died when I was very young."

"I see." He had moved to stand beside her, watching her hands move and standing with his own clasped behind his back. "And what of your father?"

"He raised me the best way he could, I believe."

"The way one would raise a prize calf for the market." His tone was as sour as week old milk.

She stopped spinning and turned to him, glaring. "My father loves me. He wants the best for me. Is there any harm in that?"

"When it puts you at the king's mercy? Yes."

Gwyneth nearly knocked her stool over as she rose and marched over to fetch another bale of straw. She was sweating as she dragged the heavy load past the dark-cloaked man.

"You will never be done in time at this rate, and there won't be time for my payment," he remarked. "I will help you to finish faster."

With a swirl of his hooded cape, he turned from her and brought over another bale of straw. He handed her bundles of straw and replaced her distaff each time it was full of gold. Gwyneth's hands flew as she fed straw into the flyer, her foot was a blur operating the treadle and the wheel spun so fast it made her dizzy. She was fairly certain the stranger was responsible for this increased speed with his mysterious magic.

Much sooner than the previous evening, or at least she thought so, although she had no timepiece with which to measure the night, the seemingly insurmountable task was finished. Rows and rows of golden thread sat on the floor. Only a few bobbins were still empty, and there was no straw left except for chaff and dust that littered the floor.

Her back stiffened as Gwyneth became aware of the stranger standing behind her. His hands rested on her shoulders, heavy and warm. She was torn between pulling away from the unfamiliar touch and purring like a cat as he kneaded her muscles lightly.

"Are you ready to pay my price?" The low rumble of his voice set her very bones trembling in a not entirely unpleasant way.

In answer, Gwyenth rose from the stool and turned toward the dark figure, ready to do her duty. She rubbed her numb and stiffened fingers against her palms, trying to restore the feeling in them. Her mind spun like the spinning wheel through all the possibilities of what he might do to her. What he did do took her by surprise.

The demon stepped toward her and took her hands in his gloved ones, turning her palms up so he could examine her cut and swollen fingers. He bent his head over them and she felt the warm, moist puff of his breath against her skin just before he pressed his lips to one palm. Her hands were hidden in the shadow of his great hood, but she felt every touch of his unseen lips as they traveled over her hands, kissing each finger, every pad of her palms and even her wrists.

By the time he pulled away, releasing her hands, Gwyneth felt no more soreness. She rubbed her fingertips against her thumbs and found the cuts from the straw miraculously healed.

"How did you...?" She stopped speaking. Having accepted the reality of spinning straw into gold, it was a little absurd to be amazed by a simple healing.

"What will happen now?" she asked instead.

His hesitation gave her the impression that perhaps her savior wasn't too certain himself now that the time for payment had arrived. He touched a gloved hand to the edge of his hood and, for a breathless second, she was certain he would throw it back and reveal his face at last.

Instead, he lowered his hand, reached beneath the folds of

his great cape, allowing her to catch a glimpse of equally black shirt and trousers beneath, and brought out a long scarf—black, of course. At first she imagined he would bind her wrists with it, then Gwyneth realized what it was for.

"Turn around," her anonymous visitor commanded, and when her back was to him, she felt his presence close behind her again. She heard the whisper of silk before she felt the cool, smooth material slip against her forehead and cover her eyes. He bound the blindfold tight around the back of her head so there was no chance it might slip down.

Gwyenth listened hard to the sounds of his movement, a slight rustling, soft breathing, the tap of boot heels, a metallic clink. What was he doing, taking off his clothing? Part of the agreement had been that she would touch him, as well as him touching her.

"It's been a long night. You must be thirsty. Drink this."

She jumped as his warm hand—ungloved at last—touched hers and pressed a flask into it. Without thought, she lifted the flagon to her lips and drank. The cool liquid that bathed her throat was unlike anything she'd ever tasted, sweet and tart at the same time and with an odd metallic tang. The deep draught quenched her thirst completely.

When she was finished swallowing, he took the container from her, his hand lingering as it touched hers again. Only after she'd surrendered the flask did Gwyneth remember the common wisdom about not drinking or eating anything from the faerie world—for certainly, this being was not of her world. Had she just done something that would bind her to him forever?

"I would see you naked." If possible, his voice was rougher than ever, so gravelly and low the words were hardly recognizable. "Unfasten your dress."

Instantly, Gwyneth's throat was bone dry again, although she'd been expecting an order like this. "I can't," she whispered.

"You promised. You must."

"No. I mean I honestly can't. A team of maids put me in this dress. The buttons are all the way up the back and I can't undo them myself." She turned and offered him her back again, shocked by her own seductive tone as she said, "Will you?"

Without reply, the man stepped toward her again and began to push the small buttons from their loops. Gwyneth concentrated on every touch of his hands on her back. He muttered something in a foreign language as he reached the halfway point, and for a moment she thought he might pop the rest of the buttons and simply tear the gown from her body. But he patiently finished the task, pulled the heavy gown down her hips and grasped her hand to help her step out of the pool of fabric. Her body felt lighter without the dress, although the horrid corset still bound her rib cage. But her bare arms were free. Gooseflesh rose on them in the cool air.

"You wear too many layers of clothing," he informed her as he set to work on her corset. "It's not healthy or natural."

"Nor is it my choice," she reminded him. "These are not my clothes any more than the gown I wore yesterday. These fancy dresses and jewels and shoes, even the undergarments, came from the king. But it was kind of him to provide them for me."

"So you like your new finery?"

She didn't really, but would not let him know that. Perhaps if he considered her as under the king's protection it would keep her safe from his advances. "His Majesty plans to make me his bride. I suppose I must get used to wearing such things."

There was a long silence and his hands stilled on the ribbons of her corset before continuing to loosen the constricting garment. "Is that what you want?"

"It would please my father," she answered.

"Would it please you?"

"Every girl dreams of marrying an important, wealthy man, having a secure future and her children provided for." She kept her answer vague. He needn't know she feared the king and found him an odious man.

"Then you shall probably get what you dream of," he remarked and continued unclothing her. The corset was cast away, leaving her unbound, her breasts rising and falling with her fast breathing.

Next he peeled off her chemise, leaving her top half completely bare. Gwyneth shivered, not from the cool air, but from being exposed to his examination. This was too similar to her naughty little fantasy about her father exhibiting her nude body to prospective suitors—awful and wrong, but oh-so-arousing.

There was another very long pause and she imagined any second he would reach out and touch her breasts, but he didn't. In the silence, she could hear his breathing and her heart beating in her ears. The prolonged agony of waiting for something to happen made her trembling worse.

"Are you cold?" His voice startled her.

"No. I'm afraid."

"I won't harm you. I only wish to look at you and...and touch you a little. That was the agreement."

"Very well, do so then." She tried to sound as cool and haughty as if she really was a queen. "I don't renege on my bargains."

What was making him hesitate? Did he perhaps feel guilty about using her so? She certainly hoped so.

And then his hands were back, loosening the drawstring of her petticoat and the one on her drawers. In seconds they were pulled down her legs and her lower half was as naked as her upper. She stood with her arms straight down by her sides, fingers clenched into fists, refusing to give in to her natural urge to shield her breasts and sex from intruding eyes. Let him gaze all he liked and touch all he wanted. Copulation had not been part of their deal, and he would not rape her. Gwyneth didn't know how she knew he'd adhere to the bargain, but she trusted he would.

Another long pause followed, long enough for her flesh to burn in anticipation of his touch. Long enough for her nipples to stiffen and her pussy to melt like candle wax. Long enough for her to leave shame at her nakedness behind and feel instead a strange thrill of pride, excitement, arousal and fear all combined in one heady brew. Long enough for her to begin to *want* him to touch her and to pine for it with every fiber of her being.

When at last he did, his light touch on the center of her belly was a jolt to her system. Her stomach muscles twitched and her shaky legs swayed. She sucked in a breath. And she realized at once that his hand was ungloved. His flesh touched her flesh.

"You are very beautiful." His voice was so hushed it seemed more a sound in her head than in her ears. "And bright. Like sunlight." His hand caressed her hair below the blindfold. Then his fingers traced her jaw line and touched her lips. "Soft."

His skin against hers was feather light, but generated so much heat she felt her flesh would burn away. Her pussy felt slippery and kept clenching hard. She squeezed her thighs together to try to gain some relief as the delicate exploration of her body continued.

His warm hands slid down her throat and chest to her breasts, lifting and cupping them. He touched the pads of his thumbs to her nipples, and Gwyneth instinctively thrust toward him. She wanted more than that slight touch. She needed him to roll and pinch and then take each nipple into his mouth.

Somewhere deep inside her, a little voice clamored that her reaction was shameful, but she couldn't deny what her body was feeling, how he aroused her and made her long for more.

Crouching down now, her tormentor moved his hands down her sides to hold her hips. His big hands bracketed her sex, but didn't touch it, which only made her crave his touch all the more. His journey continued down the length of her legs to her ankles. She knew he must be kneeling at her feet and tried to picture him that way—the large, imposing, almost threatening, dark figure humbled before her. He touched her feet and then his hands were replaced by something soft, warm and moist. Her heart nearly stopped. He was kissing the tops of her feet, first one then the other.

Before she had time to process that astonishing fact, the invisible hands moved on, sliding up the back of her calves and thighs to cup her buttocks. He let go for a moment, and she felt him move behind her, then he grasped her cheeks again, pulling them apart slightly. Her anus clenched in alarm. He was staring at it, studying this intimate part of her. She knew it as well as she knew the sky was blue. This very personal exposure shocked her, but after several moments, he let her fleshy cheeks go and continued gliding his palms all the way up her back.

Sweeping her hair aside—for it had long since tumbled down from its fancy arrangement—he bent to kiss her shoulder. Gwyneth held completely still, eyes closed even though she wore the blindfold, and felt his lips softly nuzzling the junction of her neck and shoulder. Another wave of absolute lust trembled through her. Her body burned.

"Do you want more?" he whispered.

She nodded mutely, not knowing exactly what she was agreeing to and not caring.

Once more the unseen presence moved to face her, and

suddenly his mouth was at her breast, nuzzling the underside before sucking on the nipple. The sweet, aching tug made her moan. A fine silken thread like a strand of gold tightened between her breast and her sex. Another gush of buttery warmth swelled between her legs.

His mouth released her nipple, and Gwyneth pushed her chest forward, demanding equal treatment to its mate. Obligingly, he drew the other pebbled point between his lips and rolled his tongue around it.

She would have been happy to have him treat her breasts this way for many long minutes, but once more he pulled away. Then he tormented her with another period of silence and inactivity, making her wonder where he would touch her next...and with what part of his body.

He moved away from her. She could tell by the sound of his footsteps on the flagstone floor. What was he doing? Merely gazing at her pale, vulnerable body, or was he planning something else? Her imagination went down dark paths, considered possibilities of which her virginal mind should not be aware. A slap, a pinch, a spank, the sharp cut of a whip across her breasts or buttocks—all of these images sprang from vague, murky thoughts into sharp, bright pictures. Her desire raged like a bonfire. What was wrong with her?

But her nighttime visitor did none of these. Instead, he suddenly dropped down on his knees in front of her. She felt him doing so. He framed her pussy in his hands, pulled apart the swollen folds with his thumbs—she assumed—and abruptly pressed his mouth to the erect bud at the top of her slit.

Gwyneth cried out and jerked at the intense sensation. She unconsciously reached for the head at her crotch and grasped soft hair and a hard skull beneath. His cowl was off, possibly his robe as well. But she had no time for more thought than that before the tension inside her suddenly shimmered and exploded. Her hips arched forward and her head fell back. Her legs threatened to give way, but hard hands grabbed her waist and held her upright.

One kiss on her clitoris, that's all he'd given her, and it had pushed her sensitized body right over the edge.

He helped her to sink to the ground where Gwyneth sprawled on the cool stone floor, heedless of the chaff getting in her hair or sticking to her moist skin. She groaned and arched her body once more as a last wave of pleasure throbbed through her.

As she came back to herself, her joy was replaced by anxiety again as she realized it was time for her to fulfill the other part of their bargain. He'd touched her. Now she must touch him.

She pushed herself up to a sitting position, reached up to the blindfold covering her eyes.

"No." His command halted her hand. "You will not look at me. Follow my voice."

She crawled across the floor toward him, stopped when her hand bumped against some part of his body—naked. Sitting back on her heels, she waited for him to give her further instruction.

He took her hand and held it, just held it for what seemed a very long time, rubbing his thumb lightly over the back. She wondered where he would place her hand, guessed it would be his cock. But when he finally brought it to his body, he set it against a firm, hard plane that could only be his chest. She felt his heart pumping madly beneath her palm. Was he merely aroused, or was he perhaps anxious, too? Impossible. A dark and dangerous devil like him could not be nervous.

But the thought that he might be gave her more courage. Gwyenth dared to begin to explore with her hands. She pressed them both to his chest then glided them up the hard plane to the curves of his shoulders and biceps—such bulging muscles! She stroked her hands up his neck, feeling the tendons and the pulse throbbing there. She encountered the sharp blade of his jaw and the light stubble on his cheeks. He breathed rapidly as her blind hands roamed over his face, exploring his features. His nose and the ridge of his brow, his cheekbones and jaw all felt very angular, but his lips were soft and warm. They parted as she touched them. She wondered if he was what one would consider handsome. His features seemed even and normal—no unexpected bumps or festering pustules. No horns on his head, either, she noted as she brushed her fingertips over his forehead and slipped them through the hair at his temples. What color was his hair? His eyes? Black as coal, she had no doubt.

Suddenly, he seized her wrists and pulled her hands away. "Enough. Touch me somewhere else."

"Your arms or legs? Do you mean your hands?" She smiled as she teased, amazed at herself for having the temerity to joke. She could guess exactly what part of him craved her touch, but wanted to hear him ask for it.

"Here," he said gruffly, sliding her hand down his belly—soft hair, warm flesh—to the mysterious area below a man's waist, behind the buckle on his belt. He was naked there, too.

Gwyneth caught her breath as he wrapped her hand around something thick and rigid. His penis pulsed in her hand like a living entity, and the man attached to it groaned softly. A memory rose in her mind and her lips curved.

"Why do you smile?" His voice was harsh. Perhaps he was suspicious that she laughed at his expense.

She shook her head. "I'm sorry. I'm nervous, and this reminded me of something."

"What?" he demanded still sounding distrustful.

"When I was a child, I used to love cats, but feared their tails. The way they'd twitch and lash like snakes, I was convinced they were a separate being from the cute, cuddly cats. This reminded me of that."

"A cat tail," he said flatly.

"Yes." A fit of giggles nearly overtook her as she sat there naked and blindfolded with his hard shaft in the circle of her fist. It all suddenly seemed quite ludicrous. She bit down on her lower lip as she struggled not to laugh and felt the cock in her hand diminish slightly.

"I'm sorry. I don't mean to make you uncomfortable." Why was she apologizing to the creature who'd forced her into a sexual situation in exchange for saving her? She should despise him for it, yet the sign of his insecurity touched her, and for the first time she felt a shift in the balance of power. He may have the ability to make magic and the authority to order her to strip nude, but she also had some control. She could make him feel small—quite literally.

The knowledge of her strength made her relax, and Gwyneth found she wanted to please him as he had so unexpectedly pleased her. She stroked the silky length of the shaft, slid her thumb over the moist head. She explored his member from tip to base, noting the pattern of ridged veins beneath the pads of her fingers.

There was a soft intake of breath, and his cock grew harder again. She continued to investigate below the shaft, finding the soft sac within which solid balls nestled like eggs in a velvet pouch. She forgot to be nervous at all, she was so fascinated at discovering the vast difference in anatomy between a man and a woman.

She wished she could see his cock, his entire body, for that matter, and most especially his face. Why had he insisted on a blindfold? Was he scarred and ugly, demonic in appearance, unbearably shy, or did he simply want to create mystique by not letting her see how average he was? Who or what was this man?

Her hand had stopped moving, and suddenly his hand surrounded hers, guiding her to grasp his cock more firmly. His smooth skin glided beneath her palm as her hand moved up and down.

Gwyneth's experience of sex included only witnessing the brief and fervent copulation of farm animals. She didn't know much about what happened between humans and was intrigued to find the pumping of her fist seemed to bring the dark man great pleasure. He moaned quietly and pushed into the circle of her hand.

He continued to guide her actions, showing her what he needed. Faster and faster he pumped and his low groans increased. The sound of his desire, the urgent need in it, excited Gwyneth. A new wave of arousal swept through her. Her pussy felt open and aching, yearning for something more than the pleasure she'd already received. She needed to be filled, wanted him inside her. But that wasn't part of their agreement, and she shouldn't desire such things anyway. It was wrong. Her virginity should be saved for her husband.

Heat grew between her hand and his cock as she rubbed him very quickly now. The man made a strangled sound in his throat, and suddenly, warm wetness spattered the back of her hand and wrist. He had come. She had *made* him come with only her touch, which seemed somehow as magical as spinning straw into gold. Although her sex still yawned and begged for fulfillment, Gwyneth was pleased.

He removed her hand from his cock, wiped it clean with a cloth, and set it back on her lap. Immediately, she missed the connection between their bodies. She was alone in the dark and felt dismissed. Soft, rustling sounds followed. She imagined him dressing and wanted to reach for her gown and cover her naked body.

"Are you still here?" She was ready to tear the blindfold from her eyes and find out.

"Yes. Keep the blindfold on." More sounds came from her left as he, perhaps, put on his boots and cloak.

"Thank you for helping me tonight," she said, shielding her breasts with one arm and her crotch with the other. "You've saved my life twice now."

"Will the king demand more from you?"

"My father told him this magic ability would only occur during the full moon of the fifth month every eighteen years. What possessed him to say it, I have no idea."

"The moon has not yet waned," he remarked.

"So I may be here again tomorrow night." *Will you be?*

"Perhaps I shall see you again."

"Perhaps you'll allow me to see *you* next time we meet." Gwyneth waited for a reply, but her comment was greeted with silence followed by a crack of thunder and the now familiar odor of sulphurous smoke. She pulled the scarf from her eyes to find herself alone in the room except for the rows of gold-filled spindles and the silent spinning wheel.

It took a huge effort to drag herself back to reality, to the possibility of the steward's, or even the king's, arrival at any moment. She dressed with clumsy haste, extremely difficult with the buttons up her back, then gazed at the alien cloth in her hand. The black silk scarf flowed between her fingers like water as she folded and tucked it down the neckline of her dress, deep into her bodice. She fancied the dark man himself—foreign, strange and unknowable—was pressed there against her heart.

Chapter Five

"I'm stunned," the king said, yet again. The first three times, he'd said it as he gazed in wonder around the room filled with gold thread. Now he repeated it in his ornate dining room, where Gwyneth was again eating with him—alone save for the many carefully blank-faced servants who passed in and out. Gwyneth could feel their curious stares on her face, on the back of her neck, but whenever she glanced at them, their faces were expressionless, or even averted. God knew what they thought of her, what rumors had reached them.

But there could be no doubt that the king was delighted with her.

"I'm stunned," he repeated, setting down his silver goblet. "In two nights, you've more than doubled my fortune. A third, and I doubt even the largest kingdom in the world could rival my wealth. And the beauty of it is, you'll be able to renew it in another eighteen years. Just in time for my middle age."

Gwyneth found it hard to swallow the delicacies she forced into her mouth. They seemed to taste of ashes and deceit. And the sour tang of her host's obsession with money. She began to see many similarities between the wealthy king and her poor father and realized for the first time that no amount of gold, or favor, would ever be enough for either of them.

Finally able to speak, she said vaguely, "Who knows what

another eighteen years will bring?"

"Very true. But tonight the moon is still full, and so you'll spin me another room full of gold."

She'd known it was coming. If it wasn't, she'd have been at home, berating her foolish parent. And yet her heart lurched at his words. Because she'd see her dark stranger again.

She knew she should feel ashamed of what she'd let him do to her, what she'd done to him. But the truth was, her skin burned with renewed pleasure whenever she thought of his eyes on her naked body, his lips on her "pearl", drawing such sudden, devastating pleasure from it that her pussy wept at the memory. She hadn't known such intensity was possible, and in the long, mostly sleepless hours of her day in bed, she'd acknowledged a desire to know more, much more.

It was impossible, of course. Her demon, like her desires, was wicked fantasy. Reality lay, almost as fantastically, in the king smiling across the table at her.

"I'll tell you what, fair Gwyneth," he said softly. "If you do this thing for me, if you give me this one more room full of gold from straw, I'll marry you."

Something surged from her stomach. It felt like bile.

"I'll make you queen," the king went on, as if her lack of reaction meant a lack of understanding. "The mother of my heir."

"I don't know what to say," she whispered desperately. "I'm not suited to such a life..."

"You will be trained," the king said, waving one dismissive if amused hand. He sat back on his seat, regarding her with smug satisfaction. "You have enough beauty and wit to carry it off. And let's face it, I'll enjoy flaunting you before the noblewomen who've been competing for my favors for years."

Gwyneth's heart sank even farther. "Is that a good enough

reason to marry me?" It came out more sharply than it should, but she no longer cared, and in fact the king didn't appear to mind.

"Annoying your rivals? No. Your beauty helps. And you have a certain—freshness that appeals to me. I'm told I have a jaded palate, but I shall enjoy tasting you. And then there is your great gift, which is, of course, the deciding factor."

"Of course," she repeated bitterly. She laid down her knife and gazed at him directly. "Sire, the gold is yours. You do not need to marry me to own it."

Her father would kill her for saying such a thing. Even as she said it, she acknowledged the lunacy in trying to avoid the impossibly good match being offered to her. She wasn't even sure why she did so. Some sneaking feeling that it was all dishonest, distasteful and just plain wrong.

The king laughed. "Of course I don't. But I need to marry you to have some more in another eighteen years."

"I could come to you again then..." she began desperately.

"Don't be foolish. I can't let you go, let some other man, whether commoner or king, have control of your talent."

Blood drained to her feet so quickly that she felt dizzy. She realized at last that she had no freedom. She'd been bound by her father's preposterous claims and her cheating fulfillment of them. Even if the king had released her, she'd have been sought for her supposed wealth-making talents instead of her beauty. No one would have loved her for herself. No one ever would. Unless the king came to.

She glanced at him uncertainly. His eyes gleamed within his handsome face. It might have been lust, but she rather thought it was the lust of acquisition. Could she change that?

The king said, "I'm of a mind to watch you."

Memories of the dark man watching her naked flooded her

mind and moistened her drawers. She shifted in her padded chair. "I beg your pardon?"

"I'd like to see you work. I want to see how you do it."

"Oh, no," she blurted. If he did, her demon wouldn't come, and there would be no gold. More than that, if her demon didn't come, she'd have no more opportunity to taste the delicious thrills of his caresses. Stupidly, it was the latter fear that drove the words into her mouth. "It is dull work, and in any case, I have this feeling in my bones that it wouldn't happen if anyone else were to see. More than that, Your Majesty must not be contaminated by such magic. I don't know where it comes from..."

For the first time, a flash of fear crossed the king's smug face. Was that her escape? His fear of her magic contaminating him?

He stood abruptly, and Gwyneth, too, stumbled to her feet. "You are right," he said grandly. "It is not fitting that I attend you at such work. You shall come to me in the morning with your task complete."

He held out one commanding hand, and there was nothing for Gwyneth to do but cross the floor and take it, sinking into a deep curtsy.

He smiled. "Don't be afraid, little Buttercup," he said softly. "I'll treat you well, and you shall have wealth such as you never dreamed of."

"And my father?" she managed in a strangled voice.

"Will be taken care of, naturally. Perhaps he can run the royal mills. While you run the royal nursery."

He laughed at his own joke as he raised her to her full height once more. Putting one finger under her chin, he bent his head toward her and pressed a wet kiss on her lips.

It seemed she didn't like kissing anymore. Her hand itched

to slap the king's face. Fortunately, before she could lose control, His Majesty drew back.

"Well," he said softly. "I think it will be a good deal. You have sweet lips, and I can tell you exactly what to do with them...when we're married. Now go and make me some gold."

As if he'd been lurking at the door for his cue, Wallace materialized, bowing for her to precede him.

Gwyneth walked through the door without looking back.

Wallace said to her, "You've done well, very well, for both of us. One more night, and we'll all be rich, you and me as well as the king."

"And the rest of the country?" Gwyneth said with sudden despair. If nothing else, her stay in the palace had shown her that people didn't need to live in the poverty of those she'd known all her life.

"Prosperity spreads," Wallace said vaguely. "The whole country will benefit from the king's wealth."

Was that true? Was she really doing some good? Or did she just want to calm her raging guilt? She wasn't even sure what she was guilty of any more. She just knew it had all gotten out of hand. And what she really wanted was to tell her demon so.

Soon she would have the opportunity. As she and Wallace descended the stone steps to the underground passage, her heart beat faster and faster. He hadn't kissed her mouth last night, despite the other greater pleasures he'd shown her, and now, suddenly, she was desperate that he should. After tonight, there was no guarantee she would ever see him again. After tonight, there was no guarantee she would ever know such pleasures again. She would be lost to a life of duty. A life of unimaginable luxury and wealth for which she should be prostrate with gratitude.

I'll do it. I will. I'll marry the king, and as queen I'll try my very best to look after the people. Surely there are many ways I can help, make a difference... But first, oh, first, can't I, please...?

Her desperate, incoherent plea trailed off as the door of the familiar room creaked open once more. There was barely space for the door. She had to edge into the room, so packed with straw was it. Even the spinning wheel and the stool, squashed against a high wall of bales, were almost buried in the stuff.

"Good luck," said Wallace. "And I hope you'll remember, when honors come to you, that it was I who brought them."

No, you didn't. My demon did!

Fortunately, she kept the words inside. The door slammed and bolted behind her, and she was left staring at a solid wall of straw. Laughter caught in her throat.

"This is ridiculous," she said aloud. Turning, she leaned back against the straw and closed her eyes. She thought of her previous two nights here, of the dark man's kiss, of his hands on her breasts, on her thighs, of his ecstasy-giving kiss on her clitoris. Her heated body clenched, releasing a pool of warm moisture from her desperate pussy.

One more night with him. And then, then I'll be good...

"Please," she whispered. "I need you. I *want* you."

He shouldn't have been able to hear. She wasn't even sure she meant him to. But something stirred in the room. Soft fabric, like a cloak, brushed against her forearm. She found herself smiling. Slowly, she opened her eyes, and there he stood, close enough to touch, tall and black and hooded. His familiar, faint, smoky scent filled her nostrils and her memory, feeding her galloping lust.

"There you are," she said, and reached inside his hood. His hand whipped up and caught her wrist, but she'd already found his warm, rough cheek. Mutely, she lifted her face inside the shadows of his cowl, parting her lips. She heard his breath catch an instant before she found his lips. And then their mouths met and fused, and Gwyneth drowned in sensation.

She'd been wrong. She still liked kissing, although it seemed it had to be with the demon. She must be very wicked.

His mouth opened hers and his tongue drove deep, flicking back to lick at her teeth. She caressed his cheek, slid her hand round to his head, tangling in the same soft hair she'd felt last night. With her free hand, she found his gloved one and carried it blatantly to her breast, moaning at the first touch. His fingers curled, cupping while his thumb flickered across her hard, aroused nipple. Then he moved, delving inside the neck of her gown to find her naked breast, and she moaned again as he freed it from its constraints.

The demon released her mouth and raised his head quickly to prevent her, presumably, from seeing more than the dark shadows of his face. But his hand did not leave her breast. Instead he gazed at it, as she did, watching his black gloved hand caress her palely gleaming skin, her anxious nipple rosy under the merciless attention of his finger. It seemed to stretch toward his touch every time he left it. Sparks of bliss spread downward from her breast to her pussy, gathering there while her whole body flushed with growing pleasure.

He said huskily, "We haven't agreed payment."

"I don't care. Kiss me."

He didn't. Instead, his cowl moved around the solid wall of straw. "You want all this spun into gold?"

"The king does."

"For which you'll give me..." He paused, taking a deep breath.

"Everything," Gwyneth said desperately. "Anything." She pushed into his body, glorying in the hard ridge of his cock as it pressed against her abdomen. “The king will marry me for this, for a room full of magic gold thread, spun by you. I’m lost, my angel, my demon... Give me tonight...”

He’d stilled, holding himself stiff in her hold, which didn’t suit her urgency at all. “Anything?” he repeated.

Her whole body tingled. In a web of lust and gratitude and grief that she no longer knew how to untangle, she knew she’d hold nothing back tonight. Not even the virginity that should be her husband’s. The king didn’t care for her but for the wealth she could give him and keep from his rivals. Her stranger, at least, wanted her body. That had been clear from the start.

“Anything,” she said huskily and, with deliberation, laid her hand on his crotch.

He let out a sound that was half-gasp, half-groan, and abruptly she was driven back into the wall of straw, his body hard against her.

“You give me your lips,” he ground out, crushing her mouth under his in a kiss that left her breathless. “Your delicious breasts...” He dropped his head to her exposed breast, lashing the delirious nipple with his tongue before taking it into his mouth and rolling it frantically between his lips.

Gwyneth’s head fell back against the straw, her mouth open in ecstasy.

“Both your delicious breasts,” he muttered, freeing the other for the same attentions. His lower body ground into hers, awakening deeper longings that she had no name for. Flames seemed to lick her pussy, melting it, opening it for him, so that when he began to bundle up her skirts, she emitted a little mewl of excitement.

“And this, your sex, your pussy, you would give it to me, too?”

“Yes, oh, yes,” she breathed, trembling as his fingers ran

up and down her thighs and swept inward.

"Wet, so wet," he whispered in her ear. "You are so very passionate for a virgin."

"Is that bad?" she got out, shivering under his hot breath on her skin, his fingers gliding among the folds of her pussy.

Something, laughter perhaps, shook him. "Not from where I'm standing. Will you be faithful to your husband?"

"When he's my husband, then yes, God help me."

"I don't know who to pity more."

"What does that mean?"

The finger teasing her entrance slipped inside her, making her cry out with shock and unexpected delight at the cool intrusion.

"I don't know," he said. "You take away my sanity, my determination, and all I want is to pleasure you, to make you come on my fingers..."

His palm pressed on her pussy, his thumb caressed back and forth across her swollen clitoris while his finger moved inside her, sliding up and down, probing and exploring. Shards of delight followed his every touch, building the pleasure in her core, leaving her curiously helpless as well as desperate.

"It doesn't have to be your fingers," she whispered, and for an instant he stilled. She twisted her neck to try to see his face, but the cowl was turned away from her. Slowly, his head bent toward the side of her neck and she felt his lips there.

"You want my cock?" he said against her damp skin, causing a fresh burst of wild lust. His teeth grazed her, adding to it. "You want my cock inside you, fucking you to orgasm?"

"Yes," she whispered, unable to lie. "I know it's wrong, but I do..."

Another finger joined the first inside her, and together they plunged deeper. “Oh, God!” she gasped.

“Not God, certainly not God. But it seems we both want the same thing. Only...”

She swallowed, feeling the climax begin to rise up from her toes. “Only what?” she managed.

She grasped at the fabric of his cloak, her fingers scrabbling to find purchase. His thumb tapped against her clitoris, glided over it again and again while his fingers swirled and drove inside her. “Only that is not my price,” he whispered and pressed his palm against her pussy.

Orgasm broke over her like a storm, wilder, more intense than anything she had yet experienced. She fell forward against him, and he held her, completing her joy with his kiss on her open, gasping mouth. She clung, helpless, convulsing around his fingers, overcome with profound joy that seemed to go far beyond the merely physical.

There was straw in her hair, tickling her neck, jabbing into her exposed legs. Gwyneth became aware of it very gradually as the world came back into focus. From her bodice, he was drawing the black, silken blindfold that she’d hidden there once more after the women had dressed her. She didn’t really understand why. Nor had she truly meant him to discover it, but she couldn’t be sorry. She smiled at him with lethargic, satisfied intimacy.

Deep inside his cowl, the demon’s eyes burned. A tiny droplet, like a pearl in the gloom, glistened and fell through the darkness. Only when it touched her neck, did she realize it was liquid.

Her happiness froze in a frown of incomprehension and compassion. She couldn’t bear his sadness, if that was what it was.

“What is it?” she murmured urgently. “Please...”

"It's time," he interrupted. His fingers slid out of her body, making her gasp at the sudden delight of the motion on her over-sensitized pussy. "We have a lot to do tonight."

Her skirts fell back around her legs, swished against the straw littering their small floor space. He stepped back, leaving her cold and hungry and anxious.

She said, "I haven't paid yet, have I?"

It was what gave her hope of relieving his inexplicable sadness. Perhaps he, too, recognized that they'd never meet again. She'd told him she'd be faithful to the king when he was her husband. Perhaps he, too, regretted the ending of—whatever this was. The idea made her warm and cold at the same time.

"No," he agreed. "You haven't. You said you'd pay whatever I ask."

His voice was oddly distant after the husky intimacy of only moments ago, when he'd murmured hot words into her thrilled ears.

She said, "I will."

She didn't know what he'd ask. He'd said fucking her was not his price. But whatever sexual favor he required, she was more than willing to pay. To take his sadness away, to give one perfect moment of joy as he had given her.

They still had hours.

He stood behind the spinning wheel stool, unmoving. She inclined her head and stepped in front of him to sit.

"Begin," he said, bending to lift and bundle straw into her lap.

For a time, they worked in silence. He helped her as before, bringing her the straw, removing and replacing full bobbins.

Once, she said, "What is your name?"

"My name? What does that matter?"

"I know nothing about you. I don't know your name, who or even what you are. I don't know where you live, what you look like..."

"You don't need to."

"I would like to," Gwyneth said, leaning back to let him place more straw in her lap. "You've saved my life, brought me to more wealth and dignity than even my father could ever have hoped for in his wildest fantasies. And more than that, you make me..."

"Make you what?" he prompted, but as if the words were dragged from him. As if he didn't really want to ask them.

Gwyneth stared deep into the glinting gold threads flashing past her eyes. "You make me feel what no one else does. You—touch me."

He swung away from her, pulling down the next bale of straw. "I won't touch you again."

Startled, her gaze flew after him. The wheel spun, empty of straw. *Won't you?*

Hastily, she reached for more straw. "I meant you move me."

The demon turned, dropping the bale on the floor at her feet. "As you move me. And yet you will marry the king. And I will break your heart."

Blindly, she wondered if he already had. These few days had all been so strange, encompassing the heights of happiness and depths of despair, fear and security. She'd lived in a palace by day and worked her fingers to the bone by night. And yet the nights had been her strange, dark joy. She hadn't felt the rush of fresh air or the sun's kiss on her skin since she'd come here. She suspected she'd lost all sense of reality and proportion. But right now, this dark, unknown, magical creature who made her spin faster and faster, seemed the most important thing of all.

"Where do you live?" she asked.

"In darkness."

She waited, but he said no more, merely reached across her to remove the full spindle of gold thread. She caught a whiff of his distinctive scent, and her whole body tingled from the lightest brushing touch of his arm against her shoulder.

"Do you have a family? A wife? Children?"

"No."

"What's your name?" she pleaded.

"Spin faster."

The hours passed in a blur of straw and gold thread flashing past her eyes and through her fingers. His presence, mostly silent by her side, gave her a strange comfort as well as excitement. The sadness she pushed away for another day. She would not spoil their last hours together. Instead, she wondered what he would ask of her, longed for the curious softening she sensed in him when they were physically close.

Somewhere, her demon was vulnerable to her as she was to him. She longed to give him his moment of joy, as she had done last night. And as she began on the last bale of straw, her heart began to skip faster as she wondered how it would be done.

She felt his gaze on her face, heavy, unmoving. She liked him to watch her. It made her smile, though she didn't look up from her work. It was he who closed the distance between them. She felt his touch on her shoulder, his gloved finger under her chin, turning her face up to his. Or at least up to the hooded shadows that hid his.

His gloved finger brushed against her lips with soft, aching tenderness. She kissed it. A sound spilled from him, like a groan of pain or distress, yet so faint that she couldn't even be sure she heard it.

He released her and stepped away to stand behind the wheel facing her.

"You ask my name," he observed. "But not my price."

"I've already said I'll pay."

He nodded. "Then it's time I told you what I require."

Her breath caught. Delicious anticipation flushed her body. "Tell me."

"I want your firstborn child."

Again, her hands fell from the wheel, which spun, empty. She stared at him, unsure she'd heard him right. "What?"

"Your firstborn child," he repeated.

"I don't *have* a child!"

"I'm sure you will when you marry the king. You must give the child to me."

Gwyneth closed her mouth, shook her head as if that would clear it, make his words mean something else. "Are you serious? Insane?"

He shrugged. "Serious, certainly."

"But...what do you want with a child? With *my* child?"

"You will produce a good child. Strong, just and honest. As you are."

"I hope I do," she said flatly. "And if and when that happens, it will stay with *me*."

"You promised. You owe me. And you must pay."

"No, I mustn't. It's not a price anyone can pay. It's not human!"

"*I'm* not human," he pointed out.

"I am and I won't pay!"

"You must, and I should point out that I have the means to compel you. I will come for the child. Your subsequent children will remain your own."

She stared at the still, implacable figure, feeling as if the world were falling on top of her. It was a nightmare. Suddenly, it was all a nightmare. She could not doubt the powers of the being who came and went through solid stone, who made it possible for her to spin gold thread from straw. He could and would take anything he wanted from her. From anyone, even the king.

"Spin," he said. And obediently, she did, because she could do nothing else. Her brain felt as numb as her hands. She didn't seem to move them, and yet they went through the motions of lifting and spinning the gold threads that wound rapidly around the spindle, ensuring her future.

"You tricked me. You were never going to ask for sex." She didn't mean to say the words aloud but they spilled out in a whisper, harsh, accusing. And accusing herself as much as him. She had thrown herself at him, offering herself to the demon whom she'd been determined to see as at least part angel because she needed his help and because his mysterious body aroused the lusts of hers.

"No," he agreed. "My ultimate price was determined by the first kiss. I tasted your soul and found it...suitable."

"What have I done?" she whispered. "Dear God, what have I done?"

He shrugged. "You may have saved two kingdoms."

She tried to swallow down the lump of tears in her throat, but they wouldn't go. She could no longer see the straw, the gold or the demon.

"Don't," she pleaded. "If you were ever good, please don't ask this of me."

"It's asked and promised. You must pay."

"Please!" Desperately, she dashed her fine, silken sleeve

over her eyes. "Anything else!"

"I don't need anything else."

With the last of the straw spun, the wheel slowed and stopped. Gwyneth's hands fell numbly into her lap.

The demon stirred. "Since you care so much, I'll give you a way out, but you have to find it for yourself. If you know my name by the time I come for the child, you may keep the infant."

"Your name?" She stared at him, torn between hope and outrage.

"You wanted to know it. Find it out. You have at least ten months, after all."

A way out. It was what had gotten her into this mess in the first place. But she grabbed at the proposition eagerly. How hard could it be?

With that most pressing problem alleviated, her wayward mind returned to her companion, to what they had done together and what she had offered. He had turned away from her, preparing, she was sure, to vanish.

"I'm ashamed," she whispered, hugging her sore hands to her breast like a talisman. "I believed you wanted me. I wanted to believe that. And I threw myself at you like a wanton."

He paused, without turning. "Some things we do because we want to. Others because we have to. There should be no shame in either. Not for you or for me."

He glanced back at her over his shoulder and she imagined she could see his eyes burning inside the cowl. "You need to live. I need your child. The rest...the rest was desire, both dark and sweet. And for all of it, we both must pay."

And yet you will marry the king. And I will break your heart. She hadn't understood, hadn't listened to his words. But even if she saved her child from him, it felt as if her heart were already broken, bound together only by her galloping hatred for him, beating still only through outrage at his deceit, at his abuse of her which was surely worse than the king's.

She opened her mouth to tell him so, but without warning, he erupted in front of her in a violent puff of sulfurous smoke. When it cleared he was gone. And the door of her golden cell was opening.

Chapter Six

And that was it. Those three strange days and even stranger nights were what brought her to this, to falling through heavy blackness with her child to the demon's surely terrifying lair.

On discovering his third room full of gold, the king had been overjoyed and married her with almost indecent haste. Gwyneth's feet hadn't touched the ground as she'd spun into a world of dressmakers and designers, desperate to be allowed to make her clothes and her linens, to refurbish her bedchamber and her sitting rooms. Noblemen who despised her birth had kissed her hands with elaborate respect and undressed her with their eyes. The ladies of the court watched her with envy and vied to be her friends.

Her father, now in charge of all the royal mills, had given up drinking apart from special occasions, like her wedding, and limited his boasts to "my daughter the queen." There was really no more he could say.

And Gwyneth herself had kept the promises she'd made to herself the night of her third encounter with the demon. She'd encouraged her father to diligence in his duties, had done everything she could to influence the king and bring to his attention the plight of the poor and the sick. With Midas himself, it must be admitted, she had limited success, particularly since her child had turned out to be a mere girl.

But with those ministers and stewards to whom he'd delegated, she could often arrange things more to her liking and the people's. It gave her some satisfaction to be doing some good in the end, but it couldn't fill up the void in her life. Only Brea had done that, although from the instant of her birth, Gwyneth had lived with the fear of the demon's return.

Almost as soon as she'd conceived, she'd begun her investigations, seeking out anyone and everyone who might possibly have encountered him. Remembering that the subterranean chambers, along with the one in which she'd known him, were used to accommodate prisoners, she'd sought out such miscreants who'd survived and was delighted to find two who had indeed met her mysterious dark demon. One had actually escaped with the demon's help, given in return for a box full of silkworms which the prisoner had duly delivered up. When the appointed time arrived, the demon had visited him to collect them. So she'd known he would come for her child. But neither prisoner had known his name.

Neither had anyone else. She met with tales of fleeting glimpses, of a dark figure mysteriously appearing and vanishing, although those who told the stories, fearing him or his magic or both, were reluctant to give many details.

Gwyneth had almost reached despair, contemplating flight from the king, from the entire country, to save Brea, when one of the soldiers she'd sent out to make enquiries had returned with the outlandish name, Rumpelstiltskin. And she'd been so sure, so trusting. The soldier had described him accurately, although, looking back, she'd first described the demon to the soldier when she'd sent him out looking. All he'd done was repeat her words and give her a ridiculous name to win her reward of ten gold pieces.

She should have known. She hadn't been able to imagine him dancing demonically around a campfire chanting, "The queen will never win this game, for Rumpelstiltskin is my name." Again, she'd been grasping at straws.

Terrified as she was, hysterical laughter rose up in her throat, threatening to consume her. She hadn't laid eyes on the demon from the moment he'd left her in the room stuffed full of gold thread until his abrupt appearance in the king's audience chamber. But she'd thought of him often, with both hatred and self-loathing. And in the long, lonely nights in her big, luxurious bed, she'd dreamed of him. Hot dreams full of sensual lips and hands that brought her to orgasm over and over. An unknown and mysterious figure she knew to be evil and yet whom she forgave because he loved her and pleasured her. Sometimes she woke up with her face wet with what could only be tears. And her lower body and thighs soaked with her own sexual moisture.

That was frustration, of course. After Brea's conception, the king never visited her. And even when he had, she'd found little pleasure in it. His touch lacked any tenderness, any finesse. He took and demanded, never gave. And although Gwyneth tried very hard to please him, she never knew whether she had or not.

In the end, she stopped caring. He despised her for producing Brea instead of a son. And only this morning he'd visited her to demand if her monthly courses had returned. When she nodded dumbly, he'd asked for dates and informed her that he would visit her each night of her heightened fertility period until she was pregnant with a son.

Gwyneth's heart had sunk. Not that she would have objected to another child, although Brea occupied her affections so deeply. She just didn't want the indignity of conceiving it. Another sin.

A happy marriage could not be based on deceit, could not happen without love. And neither she nor the king felt the remotest affection for each other. That, too, had brought her to this...tumbling through the air, her only anchor the hand of her captor.

When the whirling moments of freefall were over and her feet were suddenly planted on solid ground, heat and the smell of sulfur were the first things Gwyneth registered. Dry heat like that from a roaring fire on the hearth in winter, not like the sweltering humidity of a summer's day. Her skin instantly felt sucked free of moisture. Her throat was parched.

In her arms, Brea wiggled and screamed, flailing her way free of her blankets.

"Sh, baby. Sh," Gwyenth crooned absently as she jiggled her upset child. She tore her hand out of the demon's black-gloved grasp, lifted Brea to her shoulder and rubbed her back. Then she glared at the cloaked figure who'd brought her so much fear and heartache. *Don't forget the pleasure*, her disloyal mind whispered.

"Where have you taken us?" she demanded, using the imperious tone she'd learned since acting as queen.

"To my home." His voice was a deep rumble—or was she hearing the sound of rocks grating against each other?

Gwyneth looked around her in dismay. They stood in a dark cavern, which she could only guess was deep underground. The top was as high and vaulted as a cathedral. Stalactites dripped in a jagged, colorful fringe from the ceiling, some reaching all the way to their counterparts below, the jutting stalagmites that grew like thick, gnarled columns from the rocky ground. The vast chamber should by all rights have been dark, but it was lit with an eerie phosphorus glow that seemed to shine from some of the mineral formations themselves.

Beside the space where they stood rushed a dark river, which disappeared around a stony outcropping. From the other side of that outcropping, red light flickered and a hissing sound floated. A jolt of fear shot through Gwyneth as she pictured a fire-breathing dragon in the next chamber. She and Brea were to be a sacrifice to appease some horrible, underworld lizard-god.

"What are you going to do with us?" Her imperious voice quavered this time, and she clutched her squalling daughter tighter.

The demon paused. She felt him looking at her from the depths of his hood. "Do you honestly believe I would harm you?"

Despite her present panic, memories of their three nights together, so long ago now, flickered like flames in her mind—the kisses, the touches, the moments of sheer ecstasy. No. He hadn't brought her here to be some human sacrifice. And she didn't believe he was evil enough to hurt Brea, either.

"No," she answered at last. "But what are we here for then?" She'd lost all of her queenly presence.

"I will explain everything in time. Come now." He offered his hand again, but she refused to take it as she walked by his side.

He led her through the large, empty chamber, marvelous in its own twisted way. The columns of rock could have been tree trunks in a fantastic forest. She gazed in wonder at the softly glowing crystalline lights and the rippled reflections of the same lights in the water that flowed by the path.

Gathering her wits, Gwyneth cast a glance behind her at the spot where they'd arrived, noting a silver-veined slab of rock. If there was a way into this underground world, there must be a way out, and if any chance arose for her to make an escape, she wanted to know where the portal between the worlds stood.

As her escort glided at her side like a shadow, she studied the area carefully, looking for more memorable landmarks. Unfortunately, one dripping stalactite looked much like another. She tried to connect them to recognizable shapes in her mind and found one rock that looked a bit like an eagle with its wings outspread. It was near the entrance to the chamber, so she would use it to find her way back from the labyrinth of tunnels she was certain lay ahead of her.

Then her guide led her around the bend to the mouth of the cavern, and Gwyneth stopped dead. She gaped in shock at the world that spread out before her.

The space was enormous, a humongous hole in the pit of the earth. Far above, instead of the sky, was a rocky cover, but beneath it spread a land, a city made entirely of stone. Great slabs jutted up in regular intervals, and Gwyneth realized they were the fronts of buildings. Windows were carved in the stone and light shone from inside through crystals in a myriad of rainbow colors. The buildings themselves were studded with cut, polished gems that caught the ambient light and set it sparkling. Elaborate carvings also decorated the buildings.

Between the edifices were flat, cleared spaces—streets. Veins of copper, silver and gold marbled the stone. A circular fountain crafted of what appeared to be emeralds sprayed sparkling clear water. The ornate fountain stood in the center of one cluster of buildings in what must be a village green, but without the green. No grass, flowers, shrubs or trees grew anywhere in this strange, exotic world—only crystals, minerals, rocks.

But there were people—odd, unbelievable, bone-white, pale-haired people walking to and fro between the houses and businesses. A couple lingered, kissing by the fountain. A man swept pebbles and dust from in front of the doorway to what must have been a shop. An artisan was working on chipping words on a sign in foreign symbols. Vendors with carts trundled to and fro. The main source of light which illuminated this astonishing scene came from all around. At odd intervals were fissures in the rock and from those crevices flames flickered and sulfurous fumes rose.

Gwyneth gasped and cuddled her now sleepily whimpering baby to her chest. She and her child were in hell. Their captor truly was a demon.

Ragnorak cast another sideways glance at the queen as he'd been doing ever since they landed in Elohim. Why he was stealing glances when she couldn't possibly see his face within the cowl, he had no idea. But he didn't want her to know that he studied her every movement, her every expression. He didn't want her to know how much she intrigued him or how much he longed to touch her.

She feared him now. That shouldn't be a surprise. Nevertheless, it hurt when she flinched away from his touch, refusing to take his hand. What a change from the grateful creature she'd been when he had something she needed.

Now she was a queen and possessed all the riches the topside world counted as precious. Only one thing she didn't possess—her child. The little one was his now and, by extension, so was Gwyneth. She belonged to him as long as he held the girl, and he would never let the child go. She would be the heir to *his* lands, not to that ridiculous topsider king's.

Gwyneth's eyes were enormous as she beheld Elohim for the first time. He looked around at the vista before them and smiled, proud of the changes he had wrought in his world. He'd led his people from living in primitive dwellings to creating this mighty city. He'd instigated better lighting, fresher air exchange, improved sewage and water treatment. He'd inaugurated a tribunal government and court system to supplement his kingship, and he'd also copied hospitals, libraries and other useful topsider institutions, making the best the upworld had to offer available to his people.

All this he had wrought through sheer willpower, fighting against those who reluctantly relinquished the old ways.

"This is..." She fell silent, struck dumb with awe.

"It's impressive, isn't it?" He couldn't help the pride that flooded him. But it wouldn't do to sound prideful, the very aspect he detested in the topsider king. "The people have worked hard to make this city great."

"We're in hell." Gwyneth's eyes scanned the scene before them once more.

It actually took him a moment to comprehend that it wasn't awe or wonder but horror that froze her features with eyes wide and mouth open.

"This is hell," she repeated breathlessly. "And it's full of demons."

Ragnorak knew what that meant. He'd read the topsider books and understood the concept. They believed horrible, grotesque creatures inhabited the underworld to rip apart the souls of those unlucky enough to be sent there after death. Such foolishness!

He would have soothed her, comforted her, laid her fears to rest, but he was too angry and hurt. Striding forward to descend the path into the city, he beckoned her to follow with a commanding wave of his hand. "Come."

He didn't look to see if she followed. There was no place she could run to. Of course she'd stay close by him. The thought filled him with mingled pleasure—*she's mine at last!*—and disappointment—*she's only here because I forced her hand.*

Best not to examine his feelings too closely. She was here, and that was all that mattered. In time, she'd get used to it.

Used to him and the way things must be.

He might not have looked behind him, but he listened for her footsteps and heard her dainty slippers tapping across the stony ground. The child in her arms let out an exhausted whimper before falling silent at last. Asleep he assumed. He must learn more about the baby's requirements, although he felt he'd done fairly well in setting up a nursery for her. He'd assembled all the items he'd seen in human dwellings or read about in books. His golden girl should find nothing wrong with the accommodations for her child or the bedroom he'd prepared for Gwyneth—just in case she came along with them.

"What am I to call you?" she asked, suddenly near his elbow. "I think you may safely tell me your name now."

"Down here we keep our names to ourselves," he retorted.

"What? Then how do you refer to one another?"

"We have names we call each other for everyday use, but our one true name is kept a secret and only given to those who've earned the right to know it."

"That's ridiculous! I've never heard of such a thing."

He stopped, turned and stared at her. "Does every country up there have the same customs? No. Well, things are different here. A name contains power. We don't throw ours around lightly." *Especially mine,* he thought but didn't add.

"Oh." She sounded chastened and dipped her head in acknowledgement. Or maybe she just didn't want to meet his eyes. *Not that she could see them,* he reminded himself. *At some point you're going to have to reveal yourself to her.*

"In that case," she continued. "What name may I call you by?"

"Svartan," he answered. "That is what my people call me."

"Your people? You're a king?"

Of course, that was the only thing that would impress this woman, the suggestion of power or wealth. She'd fallen for it easily enough with King Midas, swallowing her pride after the shameful way the man had treated her in order to accept everything he had to offer. She was not the woman Ragnorak had estimated her to be during those three nights which he must block from his mind. Desperate to be a queen, she was as shallow as any other human woman.

Ragnorak didn't deign to answer but walked faster, leading her along the main thoroughfare. Everyone they passed stared in jaw-dropped shock at the unexpected sight of him strolling with a topsider down the streets of Elohim. He should have escorted her to the castle by a more circuitous, private route. Stupid of him to put Gwyneth and her child on display before he was ready to explain his intentions to his subjects.

At last they reached his home, which was no larger or grander than any of the buildings they'd passed. Ragnorak had made sure of that when he'd had it built. He wanted his monarchy to be understated, to be seen as a man of the people, someone who worked for the common good. That was the kind of government he believed in and was slowly establishing by setting up the tribunal, but it would take some time for the people to accept anything besides the autocratic rule they'd lived under for generations—even if their lives were improved by the changes.

"This is your palace?" Gwyneth asked as he put his hand to the knob and pushed open the iron-wrought door.

He glanced at her, checking her face for scorn, but neither her face nor voice betrayed what she might be thinking.

She followed him into the foyer, looking around at the carpet on the floor, the paintings on the walls, all lit by the crystals glowing in the wall sconces. He was proud that all the furnishings and decorations in his home were manufactured here in Elohim. None were scavenged at night from the world above as used to be the custom for obtaining luxuries.

Normally, Ragnorak would remove his cloak and gloves on his return from a foray into the topsiders' land, but he found himself nervous, not ready to expose his face to Gwyneth's stare. He paused for a moment in the hallway, then marched forward again.

"I'll show you to your room so you may rest," he said shortly.

Silent now, Gwyneth followed him up the staircase to the second level and to the room he had prepared for the baby—and for her. He'd commissioned it to be decorated all in blue, the color of her eyes. The child's cradle was made of gold, its soft bedding and coverlet woven from silk manufactured right here in the underworld. There was also a golden bed, which he would've assigned to a wet nurse if Gwyneth had not come along with him. A wardrobe, chest of drawers, washstand and mirror completed the room's furnishings. Likely not as elaborate as what she'd grown accustomed to, but overall he felt the room had a pleasing air.

Again he found himself looking for her reaction. He wanted her to be content here. But all he saw in Gwyneth's face was dismay and worry. Her brow was drawn, and she rubbed the sleeping baby's back with a nervous rhythm that betrayed her anxiety.

"Is the room not satisfactory?" He kept his tone cool, despite the stab of disappointment that shot through him.

"There are no windows. No outside light. We're deep underground." She stared back at him with a challenging gaze as if she could see into his eyes. "Brea can't survive down here, and neither can I."

She spoke to him as if he were a fool for not recognizing that obvious fact, and her easy dismissal of his world and everything he had prepared for her cut like a steel blade. Hurt feelings were a weak, human emotion—not something he had the time or patience for.

"I'm afraid you have little choice in the matter. The deal's been made. You're here now, and here you'll stay. You'll be well provided for and you *will* survive just fine."

With that he withdrew from the room before he snapped and started yelling. He closed the door behind him, breathing hard as he reined in his temper. Wild emotions rolled through him like a rock slide: anger, worry, doubt, dismay, excitement, desire. He'd planned so carefully for this day but hadn't really considered exactly how he'd deal with Gwyneth once he got her here. Or the child, for that matter.

The idea which had seemed peerless and perfect when it first dawned on him now seemed impossible and ridiculous. What was he doing? He couldn't keep the woman and child like birds in a gilded cage. And if he did, he certainly couldn't expect her to grow to love him. By doing this, he'd become no better than his ancestors who'd always stolen what they wanted from the people above, earning a reputation of evil and the name "demon", "devil" or "goblin"—all with negative connotations.

But he hadn't been able to figure out any other way to win Gwyneth or the baby he so desperately needed to be his heir. It was too late now. As he'd told her, the deal was done.

Chapter Seven

Gwyneth stared at the cold, iron door that sealed her into the rocky chamber—her bedroom. And evidently he'd known she would come with Brea. He'd intended it all along, or he wouldn't have had an adult-sized bed set up in the room along with the cradle. What was his motivation? What did he want with her?

Light as she was, the child in her arms was growing heavy. Gwyneth's arms ached from carrying Brea's sleeping weight, but she didn't want to put the baby down, to separate from her for even a moment in this dark, horrible prison.

She paced the room from wall to windowless wall, measuring the distance. Beneath her feet, a deep-piled carpet woven in swirls of blue and gold covered the stone floor. She paused by the cradle, actually a very pretty thing with its golden filigree vines and leaves. She traced a finger over the pattern and stroked the silken coverlet, but she wasn't ready to put Brea down in it.

Instead, she crossed to the bed, a counterpart to the smaller one with the same elaborate framework of leafy vines and a matching coverlet. She sank onto the foot of the bed and laid Brea beside her on the mattress.

"What have I done to us, baby?" she murmured. "What does *he* intend to do to us?"

And even now, despite her fear, despair and anger at being tricked and trapped, Gwyneth could not prevent the stab of desire that shot through her as she guessed what some of his intentions for her might be.

She fell back onto the bed, arms spread wide, and gazed at the stone ceiling. The weight of thousands of tons of earth above her pressed against her chest, making her breathing short. She felt crushed by the mere idea of how deeply buried she and Brea were. How could she escape? How could she get them back to the world of air and light?

Gwyneth must have slept because her consciousness spun back to the surface from a dark dream of frightening black beasts chasing her through winding corridors. Brea had rolled against her and was wiggling and whimpering and reaching out with her tiny hands.

Against all her husband's and attendants' objections that it wasn't queenly, Gwyneth had insisted on breastfeeding her child herself. Now milk was leaking from her breasts through her chemise and dampening the bodice of her dress. She sat and unlaced the front of her dress and undergarment, freeing her breast. She scooped Brea from the bed and held her close. The infant's little rosebud mouth latched on to her engorged nipple with a hard, toothless bite and tugged.

Gwyneth gazed into her daughter's wide blue eyes, unfocused in pleasure as she sucked hard and drank her fill. Her mind resumed scurrying the maze of thoughts that hedged her in on every side. Why did Svartan want Brea? What was his motivation in seeking Gwyneth out and helping her, only to take her child? Was this place really hell and its denizens demons? Was Svartan the Devil himself? And most importantly, how could she and Brea escape?

Perhaps it would be best to appear to capitulate rather than fight him. If he believed she'd accepted her fate, he might guard her less closely and then... Then what? Even if she could find her way back to the cavern from whence they came, how could she open the breach between the two worlds?

Hopelessness flooded her, and a tear dripped from her cheek onto Brea's forehead, making the baby blink. Gwyneth impatiently brushed the wetness from her face. Giving in to tears would do her no good.

Brea pulled away from her breast, a trickle of milk bubbling from her mouth. She reached a hand full of wiggling fingers toward her mother's face, and Gwyneth bent to capture the tiny digits in her mouth. She let them go with a loud smacking sound that Brea found fascinating. The baby's eyes crinkled in delight, and she let out a burble of laughter.

Gwyneth lifted her daughter to her shoulder and patted her back until she'd forced a few bubbles out, then switched sides. Her other breast was hard and aching, the nipple tender. She grimaced when Brea took hold, but soon the pain eased as her milk went down.

"All right, what next, little girl?" she asked her child. "Will we be brave and make the best of our new home? Maybe Mama can sweet talk mean Mr. Devil Man into seeing reason and letting us go free."

Maybe she could do more than that. Maybe she could seduce him with her body, offer herself in exchange for Brea's freedom? After all, she still had a little leverage. Her capitulating to him sexually had not been part of the deal. If he wanted her, he would have to win her. Perhaps she could lead him step by step into a new deal, making him desire her so much he had no choice but to pay any price to have her.

There was a perfunctory rap on the door and then it opened. A pale, white-haired woman wearing a black gown and white apron stood in the doorway. She stared at Gwyneth for only a moment before bowing.

"Madame, His Highness requests your presence for dinner. I am to escort you to the dining room." She lifted her head and glanced at Brea, still nursing at her mother's breast. "If you wish to change, there is a wardrobe full of gowns. I will help you and dress your hair, if you wish. And I will care for your child while you dine."

The last thing Gwyneth wanted to do was surrender her daughter into the care of a complete stranger—especially such an odd-looking one. But she'd moved past the notion that these creatures—or people—whatever they were, would gobble up Brea or hurt her in any way. Whatever Svartan had in mind for her daughter, it was greater than that.

And so she laid down Brea, who had fallen into contented sleep on her breast, in the golden cradle and let the pale woman show her the gowns hanging in the wardrobe. She reached for one at random, intent only on removing her own wet and uncomfortable clothing that would soon begin to smell of sour milk. Then she paused. Though the fabric between her fingers was a luxuriously fine silk, it was of a dull brown color and the cut was staid and unflattering. If she was to appear desirable enough to Svartan to tempt him to another deal, she needed something rather more alluring.

Letting go of the brown dress, she instead picked up a delightful golden yellow creation with a low-cut bodice. She hoped it would remind him of their nights together spinning gold out of straw.

The pale woman nodded as though satisfied and lifted her hand to unlace Gwyneth's damp gown.

At once, Gwyneth pulled away. "I can manage," she said coldly. Again the woman inclined her head impassively and stood back. While Gwyneth stripped off her old clothing and redressed in fresh, clean linen and the golden silk gown, the other woman walked to the cradle and gazed down at the baby.

Gwyneth watched her warily.

"What beautiful skin she has," the woman said warmly. "So delicate and rosy and golden...like yours."

As the woman smiled at the sleeping baby, Gwyneth realized she wasn't as old as she'd first believed. In fact, she couldn't have been many years older than Gwyneth. It was just the white hair which misled her. But all the people down here seemed to look like that. No doubt Svartan did, too.

"I have a little one of my own," the woman confided. "She's just over a year now." She looked up suddenly and caught Gwyneth's unguarded gaze upon her. The woman had pale, almost colorless eyes that made it very hard to judge their expression. "He won't hurt your baby, you know. None of us would do such a thing."

Gwyneth was conscious of massive relief. Not so much at the pale woman's comforting words—which merely confirmed what she already believed—but at the confession of having her own child. It made the woman and her people seem less like demons, and this whole world considerably less terrifying.

She pulled the laces of her dress tight and tied them with a neat bow. "What does he want with my baby?"

But it seemed the woman was finished with confidences. Her pale gaze fell away. "He'll explain it to you himself. Nothing bad for her or for you. Shall I help you with your hair?"

"It's done," Gwyneth said, dragging the brush through it several times. Taking her at her word, the woman walked to the door, opened it and called out someone's name. Gwyneth twisted her hair into a knot at the top of her head and held it with a long pin. She glanced at her daughter. "She's fed and shouldn't wake now until I return. Unless she needs changing..."

"I'll cope," said the woman dryly. "This is Karnak, who will take you to the king."

A lean, willowy man in bright red velvet, with long, white hair, bowed to her. Gwyneth inclined her head. It struck her that if she was unlikely to make friends in this world, at least she didn't need any more enemies.

"May I know your name?" she asked the woman.

"Agnet. I'm the king's housekeeper."

"Thank you for looking after Br..."

"Hush, don't speak her name," Agnet exclaimed. "You barely know me. I will gladly care for the baby until you return. Go!"

Unsure whether or not the housekeeper was laughing at her, she elected for dignity and sailed along the passage before the opulent Karnak. He fell into step beside her.

"The king will dine alone with you tonight," he said. "But I hope to have the pleasure of better acquaintance with you tomorrow."

"Thank you," she said faintly, for she had difficulty dragging her attention from his stunningly bright apparel. Becoming aware of silence, she glanced up and found his silver eyes glinting at her.

"You're admiring my suit. Gorgeous, isn't it?"

"Gorgeous is the exact word I was looking for."

Karnak grinned. "I've got an orange one, too. I keep trying to interest Svartan in something a bit brighter, but he will go for those somber blacks. See if you can't make him more..."

"Gorgeous?" she suggested, and Karnak laughed. He didn't seem remotely like a demon. "What do you do?" she asked curiously.

"I organize and arrange," Karnak said grandly.

"Social gatherings?" Gwyneth hazarded.

"N-no. Matters of government—ventilation, food, light, drainage, meetings of the tribunal."

Surprised, Gwyneth looked at him more closely. His frivolous clothing and conversation hadn't led her to suspect him of anything terribly serious, let alone worthy. And some twinkle in his strange, light eyes told her he knew it. Intelligence gleamed there, too, and in the high, proud forehead. Had her observations become too superficial in her months as queen?

But then, had she ever looked below the surface? Wasn't that how she'd been fooled by the demon, by Svartan, in the first place?

"I also have the honor," Karnak said, "to count myself among the king's friends."

Was it a boast or a warning? Or just simply information? Though unlikely, perhaps, she inclined to the last.

"And here we are." With a flourish, he threw open a door on his left and bowed for her to go in.

Gwyneth's heart was drumming. She felt as if she was taking her life in her hands, entering here alone with the demon. Part of her wanted to stay with the amusing and likable Karnak. But if she was ever to get out of here, if she was to save Brea from a life of darkness underground, she had to speak to Svartan.

Taking a deep breath, she sailed into the room as regally as she knew how.

Svartan stood by a huge, dark-stone fireplace, his back to her as he gazed into the leaping flames. His elbow rested on the beautifully carved mantle piece. He didn't wear his hood or his cloak, but she would have known him anywhere just from his all-black garb and by his stance, straight and still, poised and proud.

But his hair wasn't white like everyone else's. It was raven black and smooth, just curling over his collar. While she was still getting over the surprise of that, he turned.

Chapter Eight

Gwyneth's hand crept to her throat. She almost forgot to breathe.

Oh, yes, this was her demon. Raven hair and white skin, stretched taut over the fine, sculpted bones of his grim face. There was nothing remotely colorless about this powerful being. Instead, there was something dramatic about the contrast of light and darkness, something undeniably handsome about the hard, proud, arrogant face.

He bowed very slightly and walked toward her.

Panic rose like a tide. Oh, dear God, no wonder he was king. No one would dare to disobey this man, this demon... How could she even imagine tricking him into releasing Brea and her? Sheer power radiated from every inch of him, every confident, graceful movement of his tall, lean body. Unmasked, there were no obvious chinks in his armor. There was no faintest softness to give her hope.

As he came to a halt in front of her and peremptorily held out his hand, she realized what fascinated her about his fierce, compelling eyes. Not white or even pale gray. They were deep indigo, as fathomless as the night sky.

With a gasp of loss, she swallowed down her longing—for the overworld, for him, she no longer knew which—and forced herself to lay her hand in his. His fingers, long and thin and white, closed around it, surprisingly warm. She shuddered as memory washed over her of those same hands touching her in her most intimate places, inducing mind-numbing pleasures that she'd never known since. His gaze never left her face. She felt as if he pierced her soul, as if this was the most momentous instant of her life. And yet, when he spoke in his deep, almost sepulchral voice, his words were soothingly mundane.

"You must be hungry. Please, sit. Eat."

Trying to pull herself together, Gwyneth became aware at last of her surroundings, which had been completely overwhelmed by the vibrant presence of her host. Though not as large or as regal as Midas's dining halls, this was a fair-sized and comfortable room. Paintings on feasting themes hung on the white-painted walls. A long table, which could have seated twenty people, was set for two at one end: one at the head of the table, the other to the right. A cozy, friendly dinner, with several steaming dishes already laid out. Gwyneth recognized the smells of fish and poultry, onions, herbs and vegetables. As everything was here, it was overlaid by the same smoky, earthy scent she associated with Svartan, preventing her from picking out, until now, the mouth-watering food smells.

She let herself be conducted to the table, where Svartan held the chair on the right for her to sit before he took his own seat at the head of the table. It was all done without words or touching, which was a relief to her. She didn't think she could bear the slightest physical contact. The anger and fear she felt toward him were still too confused with memory of her previous shameful surrender to his sexual advances, with everything he'd made her feel and enjoy.

But she couldn't think of that now. Brea was more important than all her fears put together. She had to concentrate on this one vital task—freeing her daughter from the demon.

Her first association of this meal with other dinners she'd taken with another king determined to gain control over her began to fade as Svartan wordlessly helped her to small helpings from each dish. She used the time to order her mind, to calm herself and to prepare to grasp whatever opportunities she could find.

Buying more time, she at once pushed a forkful of fish into her mouth. Stunned all over again, her gaze flew to his.

"This is delicious!"

Her surprise pleased him as much as her approval. She caught it in the brief, triumphant gleam in his startling blue eyes before his hooded lids closed down and his black lashes swept over the white skin of his cheek. What's more, he'd been watching for her reaction. As if it mattered to him.

Intrigued, she swallowed the tender, tasty fish and collected a dainty forkful of vegetables.

"Where does it come from?" she asked. "Up there?"

"Down here. Fish is easy. It thrives in several underground streams and rivers. We always had a rich range of mushrooms. The other vegetables we've begun to grow quite recently. We need to create false sunlight, but we've managed to some degree. It makes for a more varied diet since trade with our world isn't always easy."

"Why not?"

He shrugged and poured her a glass of some pale liquid the color of white wine. "Our ancestors stole from yours. Your people have reason to mistrust and fear us."

She regarded him curiously. "But you trade. You've gained silkworms and other things in this way."

He took a sip of wine, regarding her over the top of his glass. "You made enquiries."

"I made a million. By statistical laws, they can't all have

been answered with lies."

"Rumpelstiltskin," he mocked. "Where in the world did you come up with that one?"

"From a greedy soldier. And my own desperation to believe," she said bitterly. Then, afraid of revealing too much when what she needed was to lull him, she swung hastily to another tack. "It must be very hard for you down here."

He laid down the glass and reached for his fork. "It's hard to move forward in any country."

She frowned, watching him place food between his strong, white teeth and chew. Without warning, her body began to flush as she remembered his mouth on hers, on her breast, her clitoris...

Don't go there, Gwyneth! Come back!

"Why don't you simply live up there?" she demanded, a little abruptly.

He blinked. "Why would I do that?"

She gazed into his half-amused eyes. "You don't want to," she marveled. "You *like* it here."

"Don't sound so amazed. Your world is as alien to me, but I wouldn't deny it has some attractions. Look for some in mine and you'll find it's not such a bad place to be."

Swallowing her doubts with some delicious garlic-flavored mushrooms, she waited for him to initiate another topic of conversation. But unlike Midas, he obviously didn't feel the need to fill all available space with the sound of his own voice. Silence rose, threatening to overwhelm her again with the impossibility of her task.

"Thank you for the gown," she babbled. "It's a beautiful color."

His lip curled. "I thought you'd like it."

She met his contemptuous gaze with defiance. "Because it's gold? You think I care for gold?"

"Correct me if I'm wrong, but I was under the impression you sold your child for it."

"I sold her for my life!" Gwyneth exclaimed, throwing down her fork. "God, that isn't right either. You tricked me. You know you did."

"You tricked yourself. Desperate to tie yourself to a rich and powerful man you didn't love, you were equally desperate to taste the forbidden fruits of desire for another man. Your people have a saying for that—having your cake and eating it, too, I believe."

Gwyneth leapt to her feet. "How *dare* you!"

"How dare I what?" He sat back in his chair, regarding her with lazy amusement. "Question your motives? Suggest an unpalatable lust you don't wish to be reminded of?"

Furious, Gwyneth tried to slow the panting of her breath while refusing to break his challenging gaze. It was his eyes that flickered first, dropping for the tiniest instant to her partially exposed breasts, which rose and fell so tumultuously.

She had it at last. The chink in his armor. It had been there in Midas's hall when she'd offered herself in place of Brea. And it was there in that infinitesimal flicker of his eyes. And now that she was looking, wasn't his breathing just a shade quicker too? Perhaps it wouldn't even have been important if he hadn't been hiding it. But his eyes were too carefully veiled, the faint smile lurking on his lips a little too fixed and mocking. He didn't want her to know.

Got you.

With the knowledge, her anger vanished more quickly than it had risen. Sighing, she waved one dismissive hand and resumed her seat. "It doesn't matter. As you said at the time, some things we do because we have to, others because we want to."

He nodded a little warily, as if suspicious of her sudden capitulation. *Good. Let him wonder, build up the tension...*

A plan was forming in her head, too outrageous to jump at all at once, but certainly deserving of some time, some mulling... Keeping her face serene, Gwyneth ate in silence.

It was a good dinner, not too rich or filling, and not too much in quantity. Brought up by a poor man to clear her plate, she had begun life at Midas's palace feeling permanently stuffed. Only with time had she learned to leave what she didn't want, and even then, she'd hated the waste like a crime against the poor and starving. Here, there was no waste. Svartan judged her appetite to a nicety, and though he civilly offered more, he didn't press her when she refused. Instead, he took her plate and his, shoving them down the long table, and replaced them with fine glass dishes into which he spooned something white and fluffy.

Watching him, Gwyneth broke her silence. "You told me before that you have no wife or children. Do you have other family?"

He shrugged. "A few cousins. A half-brother I never see. Why?"

"Are you friends? At least with your cousins?"

"We get along fine, now that they've accepted I can't be dislodged. In fact I'd go so far as to say they're loyal."

"Is that friendship?" she wondered. "Or fear?"

"It doesn't matter."

She blinked. "Doesn't it?"

"Not to Elohimese."

"Elohim? That's what you call this place? I never thought it would have a name...” Lifting her spoon, she dragged herself back to the point. “What about women? Why aren’t you married?”

“There’s no need. I have an heir.”

“Who?”

He smiled and picked up his spoon. “Brea.”

Gwyneth closed her mouth. Blindly grabbing at her own spoon, she said, “Wouldn’t your own child be preferable?”

“I’m a hybrid. I can’t have my own child.”

She would pursue that later. Although he spoke evenly, impassively, she couldn’t prevent a twinge of compassion for his childlessness. She squashed it vigorously. *Well, you can’t have mine.*

“Then you have courtesans? Mistresses?”

“I’m not a monk,” he said by way of acknowledgement.

Of course he wasn’t. Even in her innocence, she had recognized the touch of an experienced man. Excitement curled her toes. If she was wrong...

“And yet,” she observed, spooning a delicate amount of the dessert, “your behavior to me last year was not that of a sexually satisfied man.” She closed her lips over the spoon. “Mmm...”

Oh, dear God, what am I doing? What would I know? He’ll laugh in my face, and rightly so...

He wasn’t laughing. She was afraid to look, but other senses strained toward him. No sign of laughter, just a silent tension that crackled the air between them. And she could swear his eyes were riveted on her mouth as she ate her dessert with deliberate sensuality.

He murmured low, “A fuck can be more—or less—than a fuck.”

Warm blood seeped into her face at his coarseness. She was fairly sure that had been his intention, which gave her the courage—or the defiance—to look at him at last. He sat back in his chair, watching her, mocking her. And yet she could swear there was the faintest tinge of color in his own pale cheeks, that if his breathing hadn't increased there was nevertheless an air of expectation, of tension in his very stillness.

"Then," she said innocently, "your courtesans do not satisfy you? You need an extra...fillip in your encounters?"

"Do you have some suggestions?"

"As a matter of fact, yes. This dessert is really very good. So sweet and yet refreshing. What is it?"

"I'm afraid you'll have to ask the cook. It's a traditional recipe, but I've no idea what's in it."

She took some more into her mouth with delicate concentration. His eyes followed the movement of her lips, her tongue, and she was sure she'd won. And yet he didn't speak, didn't ask for elaboration.

Damn. Never mind. Can't win them all. I can afford to be generous here...can't I?

"Have you considered another game? Another deal between you and me?" His eyes held hers, an unmoving sky on a sunny, windless day.

Oh, God, I can't do this... Brea, think of Brea.

"Go on," he said evenly.

"I'll give you another three nights," she said, ignoring the growing heat of embarrassment in her body. Not lust, not now, how could there be ever again? "I'll freely share my body with you, experiment with whatever pleasures you choose to explore. But if you orgasm in that time, Brea and I must be set free."

He stared at her, deep into her eyes, never moving. He didn't even seem to be breathing. *I've gone too far.* Now *he'll laugh in my face.*

His full lips parted. “And if I’m able to resist your charms and maintain control over myself?”

“We will stay here and you will never touch me again.”

A moment longer, he held her gaze. “Worst of all worlds for you. No freedom, no sex. On the other hand, if you haven’t managed to bring me to orgasm in three nights, it isn’t likely I’d *want* to touch you again.”

He was trying to humiliate her, make her back down. The knowledge helped her deal with it, though she couldn’t prevent the burning in her face, the indignant tightening of every muscle.

“Afraid to play this time?” she challenged. “Because you don’t hold all the cards?”

His gaze dropped, as though considering.

Oh, God, what am I doing? I don’t have the skills to please an experienced man, let alone an experienced demon! Besides, he already has us in his possession. Why would he make such a deal?

But I know him. I do. And I have imagination. More than that, he wants me. I know he does...

His gaze came back to her. A smile played around his lips, seeped into his hard, dark eyes. “All right. I’m amused. But I have some conditions before I make the deal.”

“Name them now, and I’ll consider them,” said Gwyneth, who had learned a lot from her previous mistakes with this being. The gleam of his eyes acknowledged it.

“Very well. Two conditions. First, a time limit. On each occasion, you have two hours in which to...ah...do your worst.”

Gwyneth nodded. Two hours was more than Midas ever spent with her at a time. She was pretty sure it was more than the demon himself had spent in any intimacy with her, even on the second night, although of course she had no proof of that...

"But," she added, innately suspicious. "You can't have any kind of sexual relief immediately before our two hours begin, either."

His lips twitched. She was definitely amusing him. Flushing, she nevertheless lifted her head in defiance. But it wasn't easy. Svartan had always been a powerful physical presence, even in his mysterious cloak and hood. Now, with his dramatic black hair and pale skin, and his intense, mocking eyes, he was overwhelming. She couldn't help but be aware of his sheer size, the breadth of his strong chest and shoulders, the arm muscles bulging through his black silk shirt sleeves. She'd touched his body, so warm and hard and smooth, corded muscle and sinew rippling under her questing hand.

She swallowed hard, desperately trying to refocus her mind on the deal. If he tricked her again...

"How long is immediately?" he enquired.

"Twenty-four hours," she said in a rush of relief. With any luck that would invalidate tonight, for although she was so desperate to escape, she wasn't anywhere near ready yet for a sexual encounter with him. She needed time to think, to prepare, to gather the strength and the courage to do what she had to.

"You are a hard negotiator," he observed. His voice, his gaze, remained steady, and yet she couldn't rid herself of the notion that he was still laughing at her.

"From you, I'll take it as a compliment," she retorted.

He inclined his head, as if that was what he'd intended. "I accept twenty-four hours."

"Then I accept the two hour time limit. What is your second condition?"

Reaching forward, he picked up his glass and sipped the wine while he appeared to consider. Gwyneth wasn't fooled. She knew he'd already thought of it. "That I choose the nights."

"What?" She floundered for composure.

"I choose which nights we spend together. " His impassive face gave nothing away.

"No," she said abruptly. "You could drag it on for months, for years. I won't wait that long for the chance to free my child."

The black eyelashes swept down over his pale cheeks and rose again almost immediately. Again, he inclined his head. "Then we can put some time limit on the whole deal. What would be acceptable to you? Three months? Two?"

"One," she said quickly. *Damn, why didn't I say a week?* And yet she needed time to do this properly. You just had to look at him to know this would not be an easy solution. So, for Brea, she could wait one month.

A month in hell...

The demon said, "Then it's a deal." Gravely, he stretched out his right hand. Gwyneth's heart hammered in her breast so loudly it should have disturbed the entire underworld. There was an instant of terror at what she was doing, making another deal with the unearthly, surely ungodly creature beside her. And such a deal!

But it was fitting. She had been defeated and brought here at least partly because of her own desires. Let her triumph this time through his.

Slowly, she took his hand, felt the firm, warm grasp of his fingers. Lightning sparked up her veins, even now that she knew what he was. *Do I?* she thought wildly. *Do I really know that?*

The deal was done.

The demon let her hand slide away and smiled. “I choose tonight.”

Chapter Nine

Under Wallace's anxious gaze, Midas strode back and forth across the room, snarling questions. He knew he was too furious to think straight. He was lashing out, refusing to believe in anything more powerful than himself. His gold-spinning wife had been stolen by a trickster, a magician, a charlatan who would pay with his life. Just as soon as Midas's idiots found the bastard.

"Yes, sire," Wallace assured him once more. "The whole country is being scoured, but there is simply no trail to follow." The steward took a deep breath and spoke in a rush. "Sire, we cannot follow into the magical realms…"

"Magical realms?" Midas spat, stamping his foot in rage. "What rubbish are you talking now? A stupid piece of trickery, of showmanship, doesn't make him magical!"

"Of course not, Your Majesty," Wallace said at once, so humbly that Midas was infuriated all over again, rounding on Wallace with all his anger as well as the fears he'd been refusing to acknowledge.

"What is the matter with you? Can't you ever tell me I'm talking complete and utter bollocks?"

Wallace trembled visibly. "No, sire," he managed.

The king sneered at him. "Afraid I'll sack you, execute you, ruin your family?"

"Yes, sire," Wallace said truthfully.

The king curled his lip. "Not surprised. But you're right. I *am* talking bollocks." He pounded his closed fist on his forehead. "Damn it, I can't pretend the paralysis of my court and the men-at-arms was due to mere surprise. He couldn't be anything *but* magical, could he? There's no earthly way he could have vanished like that, leaving no trace, taking Gwyneth..."

And now that he'd said the words, admitted the possibility for the first time, a host of memories flooded his mind. Terrifying tales told by his nurses when he was a child, servants' superstitious words placating evil that he'd half-overheard and ignored throughout his privileged, protected life. He should have paid more attention. But then again, that's why he had servants.

"What do you know of elves and demons, Wallace?"

"Nothing, alas, beyond the stories everyone knows and educated men didn't believe. Until now, when we saw..."

"It's true, isn't it?" Midas said, not quite understanding his certainty now when only moments before he'd been so vociferous in denial. "There *are* magical realms. There is a world below ours, a world of darkness and magic. He's taken her there, and I must have her back."

Where had that come from? Servants' chatter... Memory stirred, one more important and more definite than all the other fragments.

Wallace interrupted his efforts at retrieval. "He said he wouldn't hurt the child."

"I mean Gwyneth," Midas snapped. He drummed his fingers on the back of the nearest sofa. "How do I know this? How do I know the magical realm is below us?"

The hazy image of his dying father chose this moment to invade his mind. The old king, white-bearded, weak and delirious on his death-bed, clutching his arm and spilling nonsensical stuff into his ear, about a youthful liaison with a demon princess.

Midas hadn't wanted to be there. They'd made him go and he'd been surly and resentful, an emotion hardly challenged by his father's insane ramblings. He hadn't listened at the time and he certainly hadn't thought about it since, but what if his father *had* known something?

"Wallace," he said slowly, "you served my father, didn't you?"

"I had that honor."

"Did he ever talk to you about some affair with a demon princess?"

"Certainly not," said Wallace, clearly affronted by such impropriety. Then, after an instant's hesitation, he added, "Though there was an affair, before his marriage. The older courtiers talked about it when I was young. Some mysterious woman who gave birth at the palace and then vanished with her child. Or was sent away. Opinions varied as to what happened to her, but neither mother nor son was seen here again."

"Son..." Midas repeated. Yes, the old man had mentioned a son. Midas's own half-brother, who would be king of the underworld one day... Insane words of a dying man, barely remembered after ten years?

Excitement began to replace his helpless anger. He was on to something, he was sure of it!

"How did he meet this mystery woman?"

Wallace shrugged. "Alone. He used to go walking alone at night. He was strong-willed in his youth and no one had been able to prevent him or accompany him." He gave a quick, apologetic smile. "Apparently the servants swore she was a fairy princess. The court tended to the belief that she was a low-born strumpet. Certainly, there was never any talk of marriage, and the child was never acknowledged. Perhaps it wasn't even the king's."

"Must have been," said Midas. "Why else would he have let it be born here? Wallace, go and track down some of those old servants. Find out if anyone knows any more. Perhaps somebody saw her go. Perhaps somebody knows the way to the magical realm, and then we'll get the queen back."

"And the princess," Wallace reminded him. Midas dismissed that with a wave of his hand. He had no objection to the baby coming back, but it was his gold-spinning wife he needed.

As Wallace left to do his bidding, Midas sank onto his day-bed and lay with one arm flung across his eyes, as if shutting out his everyday world would more easily bring back that barely-regarded night so long ago, the night the old man finally died and made him king. What *had* he said about the child?

Silly old twittering fool, his breath stinking, his crusty beard trailing across his arm as he blabbered on... "He'll be a king one day, too, you know...a mirror of you... A king of the demons...if he's ever strong enough to wrest control from the warring factions who live there."

Yes, he was sure those were the words, or something like. And then...hadn't he gone on to insist that Midas might one day need this demon king's help? If Midas wasn't mistaken, he'd laughed out loud at this and tried to pull away, having grown bored even pretending to listen. The old fool's words were penetrating anyway, and Midas's dreams of possessing power and riches greater than any monarch's in history were being annoyingly interrupted.

But he had cause to be grateful for the penetrating nature of those words now, because Midas was sure he did need them. If he really existed, he needed that demon brother's help *now*, only how in hell did he find him?

"Just say his name," the old king had whispered, clinging like a leach and dragging Midas down to his papery lips that felt dead already. "Say his name and he's got to come, His name is..."

What *was* the name the old man had whispered into his offended ear?

Damnation, he couldn't remember. Not even a letter. Midas doubted he'd even heard it. He'd been too busy wishing the old codger would just hurry up and die. How could he have known the ramblings were real, that there really was a magical realm, or that he would one day need to command the help of this demon brother?

Midas sat up and swore fluently. If only he'd paid attention to the name.

If only his stupid cow of a wife hadn't seen fit to abandon him for the child. If only she hadn't been damn foolish enough to make deals with demons in the first place, which is what their conversation seemed to imply to him. If only she hadn't been so scared or secretive or whatever that she'd kept the information to herself and imagined she'd actually come up with the fellow's real name.

What *was* that name his father had spoken?

One thing it wasn't was Rumpel-bloody-stiltskin.

Chapter Ten

"Do you love your husband?" Ragnorak asked. He hadn't meant to, not directly, but it slipped out when he'd closed his bedchamber door and realized she was trembling. She wasn't as hard as he'd been imagining, and yet neither did he wish to imagine her as devoted to the topside king. What would that make him?

She shook her head, moving away from him. "No. Nor does he love me."

"And yet, you are desperate to go back to him."

She smiled, a slightly twisted little smile, but at least it was genuine. "No, not to him. To fresh air and sunlight. And freedom. I won't go back to the king."

That did surprise him. "He's your husband." Had he really said that? He sounded like a prude, which was ridiculous after the deal he'd just made with her.

"Not for much longer. I'll divorce him."

Ragnorak blinked. "Will he let you?"

"He will when I tell him the gold was a lie. He's seen you now. He'll believe me. He might even have worked it out already that I didn't do the spinning."

"So what will you do?" he asked, fascinated in spite of himself.

"I'll take Brea—you might have noticed he isn't exactly an adoring father—and live in a cottage where the wrens nest on my roof and crap on my porch. And this time I'll love it because I have Brea and I know the alternatives."

"You have it all thought out. Next you'll realize I've done you a favor."

Her eyes flickered up to him, surprised and frightened. Something like laughter caught in her throat. "Not that," she said fervently.

She looked away at once, but he closed the distance between them and reached for her. Though she flinched, he didn't draw back, but simply took her chin in his fingers and turned up her face to his. He read a desperate courage in her eyes, a determination barely clambering its way over her fear.

This isn't how it should be...

Sparring, negotiating with her had been fun. Watching the color ebb and flow in her beautiful, golden face had been alluring as she'd made her outrageous deal. Inspiring some kind of fear had seemed a reasonable return for his months of secret heartache, and yet now that she stood before him, doing her best to hide it, he didn't like that fear. He wanted to dominate her. He wanted to win her. But despite all his planning and everything he'd done, he didn't care who won this ridiculous contest, as long as he had the time to touch her heart first.

Holding his gaze, she caught her lip between her teeth, as if to cover its trembling.

That first kiss in Midas's dungeons had been true. If material greed had contaminated her—and actually, he doubted it at all now—the damage was not deep. And in any case, he found it didn't matter. The ache had begun again the moment he'd looked at her in Midas's hall. And in his own, he'd been forced to admit it to himself. Although the sexual tug was strong, it was something deeper which drew him to her.

He didn't want her to feel like an adulteress while she seduced him. He didn't want her to be afraid of him. It made him feel like a rapist, whoever was in control of the night's events.

"We seal our deal with a kiss," he said softly, and took it before she could object. But he made it gentle, tender, soothing her agitated mouth without too much invasion. Her lips were nectar, sweet and soft, just as he remembered them. He sensed her surprise and left it there, before temptation to deepen the kiss overwhelmed him. "And now our two hours begins."

He moved away from her casually, saw her blink and begin to take in the appearance of his room—the desk at which he often worked during the night or in the early hour of morning, piled high with papers in neat piles. The soft rug under her feet, the fine paintings on his wall of many of the beauty spots of Elohim—the Purple Caverns, the Stream of Light, the Fire Pool.

He sank down on his large bed with its pure white silk coverings and sprawled there, watching her with his head propped up on one hand, and waited for her to approach him.

She did, slowly. A pulse beat in her throat. Uncertainty, even fear, remained, but he dared to hope there was a little excitement in there too. The carefully filtered light coming from either side of the room caught the gold of her gown, dazzling him with visions of golden thread and a pliant, willing body trembling with passion in his arms.

But she would not be so easy to resist if he let his memories go there. Thrusting them aside, he watched her climb on to the bed and gaze for a long moment at his crotch.

Partly, it might have been a fear of beginning. Partly, he suspected she could see right away what her gaze did to him. Already perky just from being with her, his cock began to grow and harden in earnest. Well, that was all right. No one said he couldn't be aroused. It was going to be a sweet two hours of torture.

Without so much as glancing at his face, she reached for his buttons and began to undo them, one by one.

He said, "By the laws of Elohim, if either party in a marriage announces their divorce three times before a witness, their marriage is dissolved."

Pausing on the last button, she took a moment before she glanced up at him. "Then I divorce Midas." She slipped her hand inside his trousers, and her fingers brushed against his still covered but highly sensitive cock. "I divorce Midas." Deftly, her fingers pushed aside his undergarment, and he found himself holding his breath. "I divorce Midas."

Her palm wrapped around his cock and he almost groaned with the ache of pleasure. He'd longed for her touch for so long, he feared he'd lose the bet right then. She leaned forward slightly, granting him a glimpse of her beautiful heavy breasts within the golden gown, as she freed his cock.

"Then you're a free woman," he managed. "So do your best to make me come."

She stroked him and he knew immediately he'd made a big mistake by demanding they begin the contest tonight. He was already wound tight, desperate for her. The smart thing would have been to wait several days and make sure he'd relieved the worst of his desire by his own hand before he allowed hers on him. Not to mention, if he intended to win Gwyneth's affection, he should at the very least have given her a night of rest and time to acclimate to the abrupt change in her life. So foolish of him to rush right into the touching and kissing that would surely undo him. But from the moment her offer had left her lips, his blood had rushed straight to his cock and that appendage had spoken for him. Now he must control the damn thing before it cheated him out of his hard-won future.

The simple sight of her hand encircling his pale shaft sent a jolt of lust through him, never mind how good it felt. He concentrated on breathing, in and out slowly to decrease the rapid thrumming of blood through his veins. He would concentrate on Gwyneth, the shape of her face, the texture of her hair, the changeable nature of her eyes, to distract him from his body's reaction to her.

Her eyes were as blue as the lapis lazuli pools in the amethyst-studded Purple Caverns. The vibrant blue stones were what gave the clear pools of water their astonishing color. Ice cold water—a good thing to think of right now because Gwyneth's hand was moving up and down his cock in a tentative glide. He shifted restlessly, trying not to enjoy it too much, which was, of course, impossible.

He studied the slight frown of concentration between her brows. She acted uncertain. With a stab of jealousy, he wondered about her experience with her husband, a man she didn't seem to care much for. Well, they'd managed to produce a child, so they'd clearly had sex on occasion. A bolt of white hot iron shot through him at the mental picture. He didn't like the idea of his golden girl with anyone other than him. For the past year and a half the knowledge that she was with Midas had burned beneath his skin. But now she was his, and would remain his if he had to cut his cock off to avoid coming—although that would rather defeat the purpose of having her.

He smiled at the thought.

Gwyneth glanced at him and her frown deepened. "Am I amusing you?"

"It was nothing, merely a passing thought. Pray continue."

Was she pouting? Her lower lip jutted slightly and he longed to bite it. So, he'd hurt her feelings a little, maybe caused her to doubt her ability to arouse him. That was good. Keeping her off balance and unsure of herself was exactly what he needed to do. If she realized she held him in the palm of her hand, he'd never make it through this evening.

"You're doing fine," he assured her in a casual, nearly bored tone that betrayed none of his inner excitement. "Really."

Her hand stopped moving on his cock, then let him go as she sat back. The same hand moved restlessly against her chest, plucking at the ribbons lacing her bodice. "Perhaps you would like other stimulation first."

She rose from the bed and began to undress.

Ragnorak swallowed and his jaw clenched. This was going to be so much harder than he'd thought. He risked losing everything, both her and his heir, for the sake of what? A few nights of pleasure that would actually be torture since he couldn't come. What a ridiculous, stupid bet to make! He could have earned Gwyneth's trust and maybe her affection given time, sweet-talked and seduced her until she was glad he'd brought her to his underground kingdom. Now he was trapped in a situation that guaranteed he'd lose her even if he won, for if she stayed here he'd promised never to touch her again.

He wanted to close his eyes, refuse to watch her slow stripping, but could not force himself to look away as she unveiled her body in tiny increments. The sloping curve of her shoulders. Her arms bared. The dress falling to the ground in a drift of gold. White ribbons of her corset parting. The full swell of her breasts revealed. A delicate tracing of blue veins marbling the creamy skin. Her nipples, dark and distended.

Her breasts looked different than the last time he'd seen her naked, and he suddenly realized why. She was nursing the child. The realization struck him like a slap to the face, breaking through the haze of lust. She was a mother with an infant. She was nurturing a life which he'd threatened to take away from her. How could she ever feel anything but horror and revulsion for him?

But his lapse in lust proved brief as she pulled her petticoat down to reveal the cradle of her hips and the tuft of tawny hair that marked her sex. His arousal was full blown once more, his erection lifting of its own accord at the sight of her plump, pink pussy lips below the tangle of curls. If his cock had a voice, it would be screaming, “Want. In. Now.”

Down, boy. He glanced at the hourglass by his bedside, which he’d placed there at Gwyneth’s command since he possessed no clock. Time was measured differently down here with no sun or moon to mark the days. Its passage was based on an inner sense of the earth’s natural cycles, a sort of deep pulsing within the field of gravity that the Elohim felt in their very bones. Ragnorak didn’t really need to look at the grains of falling sand to know there was still an hour and a half to go in this torturous contest of wills.

Gwyneth followed his glance to the hourglass but took her time as she sauntered slowly back to the bed. If he’d made her doubt her technique or her ability to please him, she didn’t show that misgiving as she sat on the edge of the bed beside him. She bent to the task of pulling off his boots. He helped himself out of his trousers, and then she unbuttoned his shirt.

Ragnorak leaned forward, allowing her to pull it off his arms before reclining against the pillows once more. Unfortunately, her chest was level with his eyes and the sight of her turgid nipples and swollen breasts made him swallow hard.

She must have noticed his convulsive swallow because she leaned forward so her breasts were a breath away from his face. “Taste,” she commanded in a low, throaty whisper.

His mouth opened obediently as she guided her ripe breast to his lips. He closed his lips around the distended nipple and drew on it hard. Warm softness filled his mouth and then sweetness burst on his tongue. He swallowed. Milk. Holy gods, he was drinking from her! It wasn’t what he’d intended or expected. But the knowledge that he was taking in her life-giving fluid was shockingly erotic. He sucked harder.

Sliding one hand around her waist, he held her while his other hand cupped her heavy breast, feeling its weight and texture and the moisture that dripped from her nipple.

Ragnorak stopped sucking, pulled away from her with a catch of his breath and looked up into her face. "You're... Do you need to feed the child now? I didn't think to ask you before we started."

She gazed into his eyes. Hers were now a dark indigo, the pupils dilated and her expression hungry. He was comforted that she was aroused too.

"Brea should be all right for a while longer. I fed her just before dinner."

Brea, his heir. He'd hardly given any thought to the baby as a tiny being with a life of her own. All of his focus had been on winning the child and her mother. He hadn't considered the baby's needs, leaving the acquisition of supplies for the nursery to Agnet. Now, for the first time, he truly understood the magnitude of adopting the child as his. She was real. She was alive and totally dependent on others to care for her. He'd scarcely looked at her yet, but he would remedy that beginning tomorrow.

Glancing at Gwyneth's other tit, he unconsciously licked his lips. "But you're... leaking. Doesn't that mean something?"

"It happens sometimes when I'm excited, not just when Brea needs feeding." She smiled. "I'm a fountain right now."

He inclined his head, accepting her explanation and the admission that she *was* excited, then he took her other breast into his mouth. As he suckled the warmth and sweetness, he toyed with her free nipple and stroked his other hand over the curve of her ass, feeling her silken flesh.

Gwyneth was busy with her own hands. She curled her fingers in his hair, holding his head to her breast. Her other hand traced a path from his shoulder, down his chest and stomach to his groin. Once more she encircled his erection and pulled.

With a grunt he pulled away from her breast and clamped his teeth together, resisting the overwhelming urge to surrender to passion. He felt like a youth, prone to spilling at the mere thought of a woman. What had happened to his ability to control himself? Gwyneth spun him around with a touch and made him lose his sense of purpose. The primal desire to bury his cock inside her was all that filled his mind.

As she moved down his body, kissing the path her hand had traced from chest to belly, he gazed at her golden hair shrouding her face. So bright. So sunny. Not that he'd ever seen the sun except at an oblique angle. His kind couldn't bear its bright rays.

Her soft, silken hair trailed over his skin, tickling softly, making his stomach muscles twitch. Gwyneth pushed the curtain impatiently over one shoulder so he could see her lovely face as she lowered her mouth to the tip of his cock.

Ragnorak bit his lip and held his breath.

She looked up at him, met his gaze as she drew his foreskin back and wrapped her lips around his flushed head. Heat and warmth surrounded him. Her tongue slipped around the shaft, stroking, soothing, firing him up.

He gasped and thrust toward her.

Control. She had it. He was losing it more and more with every tug of her hand and slurp of her tongue. And now she was drawing him deep. His head bumped the back of her throat and she moaned, the vibration shooting up his shaft. He felt like his groin was on fire. His balls drew tight. He trembled with the need to come. And she'd barely begun. No way could he hold out for another hour. If he couldn't bear a simple blow job, how would he fare if she decided to straddle him and slip that velvet pussy onto his cock?

He reached out and touched her head, combed his fingers into the smooth, cool strands of her hair. Her scalp was hot underneath and her head moved up and down as she swallowed his cock.

Lose it and she'll be gone, he reminded himself. A couple of hours is nothing against a lifetime of having your heart's desire—a wife and child of your own.

The reprimand helped a little. Very little. For now she was cupping his sac, fondling his rock-hard balls and teasing one finger along the path to his anus. His opening clenched in anticipation of her touch. But she never reached that far.

Abruptly, Ragnorak, clenched his fingers in her hair and pulled her off him. "Enough!" He wasn't rough, didn't pull her hair, but tugged gently. Was he breaking the deal by not allowing her to finish the job? He didn't care.

The only way he could win would be to concentrate on her pleasure, her body, not his. Everything depended on his being in control. And so he pulled her up beside him and flipped her onto her back. He lay on top of her, his cock nudging insistently at her entrance, and he kissed her.

Hot and deep he probed her mouth, tasting a trace of the wine from dinner and the indefinable something that belonged to Gwyneth alone. He wasn't inexperienced at kissing, but with her it felt completely different—new and amazing. What was it about this woman whom he barely knew that stirred him so? Was he as shallow as Midas, merely coveting her great beauty? But no, there was something more. Something inexpressible about his feeling for her.

After several moments of deep kissing, he abandoned her mouth and moved to her throat, lapping the precious salt from the dip between her collarbones. He kissed her chest, nuzzled the underside of each breast but ignored the nipples this time and moved lower. Her belly was taut, but still somewhat curved from having carried a child. He swirled his tongue into her navel, and her stomach flinched.

He spread his hands over her hips, pinning her to the bed, and he moved lower, skirting around her pussy, bestowing nibbling kisses to the soft junction of her legs and abdomen. Lower still, he roamed. Between her legs now, tickling her inner thighs with his tongue.

Gwyneth moaned and shifted beneath his hands and mouth. A surge of triumph rolled through him. He was back in control. Sure his dick was as hard as hematite as he pressed it into the mattress, but although it might be leaking a little, he wasn't coming.

However, he would make certain Gwyneth did.

He slid his tongue lightly up her seam, sampling her musky juice. She squirmed beneath his restraining hands on her hips. He took a moment to simply view the erotic sight of her plump pink folds, open before him. Then he dipped his head and flicked the tip of his tongue over her clitoris. This time she didn't just wiggle, she jerked.

Ragnorak pulled away, giving her time to consider the intense pleasure he could give her. He returned to kissing her smooth inner thighs all the way down to the backs of her knees. Oh, yes, he could keep this up for the rest of their time together. Teasing her, bringing her to the edge of climax then backing off. He was a master at that.

And so he began his torture. He lapped at her clit until she shuddered then abandoned it again, leaving her whimpering. He slid his fingers into her entrance, testing the tightness of her slippery channel with slow thrusts. Just as she fell into a rhythm, rising to his thrusts, he stopped that and moved on to a different stimulation. He nipped her swollen pussy lips, sharp little bites intended to give just enough pain to make her gasp and writhe. Then he licked the tender flesh, soothing it with laps of his tongue.

Back to her clitoris again. He swirled his tongue around the erect bud then gave her an unexpected nip. She yelped and her hips arched off the bed. Reaching beneath her, he grabbed hold of her buttocks and held her firm while he went to work on her, licking insistently over her clit until he could tell from her panting and thrusting that she was on the very edge.

Once more he left her there, teetering at the precipice. He moved his face lower, slipped his tongue inside her and lapped her cream. His poor, aching cock was weeping in earnest. He rubbed against the silken sheets, trying to relieve himself with a bit of friction, but not too much. Time was speeding past and soon the top of the hour glass would be emptied. He'd distracted Gwyneth from her mission, made her so hot and aroused she'd lost track of time.

Again he returned to treating her clit. A quick glance at the glass assured him it was safe to let her come at last. He grasped her hips and bent to his task again. Her skin was moist beneath his hands and trembling from tension. He would give her the release she craved.

Gwyneth whined and moved beneath him as he lapped her once more. He felt powerful as he drove her to her conclusion, bringing her once more to the edge and pushing her over. He knew when she'd taken the plunge because she cried out, a wonderful, full-bodied wail of delight. The sound thrilled him and filled him with pride. He'd made his angel soar.

He tensed his thighs, dug his cock harder into the mattress and kept his mouth latched onto Gwyneth's clit until he felt the last spasm pass through her. Only then did he pull away, pausing to wipe his mouth on her thigh.

Ragnorak regarded the expression of ecstasy on her beautiful face—open and vulnerable and alive. He'd given her that. It was what he wanted for her always. Pure joy. He dreaded her return to her senses, when she'd open her eyes and regard him again with dread and mistrust, but he couldn't fault her for that. He'd earned her suspicion and fear.

He pushed himself upright, resting on one arm and still watching her face. And just as he'd predicted, Gwyneth's eyes opened and her expression closed like a house with shuttered windows. The delight was doused and wariness returned.

Her gaze flew to the timepiece in which the last grains had long since fallen. Then she looked at him. Despair bloomed in her eyes. "You tricked me."

"No, I didn't." The fact that he spoke the truth didn't relieve his sense of guilt. She'd allowed herself to be distracted. The blame was hers, but still he felt like a criminal. It didn't make sense.

"No. You didn't," she agreed dully. "I was a fool."

"You have two more chances," he reminded her, trying to appease. "Better luck next time."

She narrowed her eyes and rose from the bed to gather her clothing. In moments she was dressed. "May I return to my room now?"

Ragnorak had risen, too, and he rang the bell to summon Karnak.

"I'm sorry things didn't work out as you wished." He heard his cool, distant tone but couldn't seem to do anything to warm it. No wonder she hated him. He was as approachable as a block of marble.

He pulled on his dressing gown and stood in silence with arms folded until Karnak arrived to escort her to her chamber.

"I will see you tomorrow at breakfast and explain more

about my intentions for you and your daughter."

She nodded curtly, not deigning to answer, and turned on her heel to follow Karnak from the chamber.

The moment the door closed behind them, Ragnorak collapsed onto the bed. He threw himself back, allowing his robe to fall open. Before their footsteps had faded, he had his cock in his hand and was rubbing himself to climax with hard, rough pulls. It only took a few moments and it was as unsatisfying as it was brief.

His tension was relieved, but his desire remained unabated, swirling inside him like a whirlpool. He wanted her more than ever, needed to win her over, and with two more engagements to go he despaired of making it through another such session without coming.

Ragnorak wiped the spunk off his stomach and lay there with an arm covering his eyes. The worst of it was that even if he won the bet, he might not win the lady. In the next few days he must convince her that he was a kind, decent, honorable man and not a demon. But how could he convince her when he wasn't even sure of it himself?

Chapter Eleven

She'd failed to make her captor come. Now she had only two more chances. What was the matter with her? How hard was it to bring a man to orgasm? She'd managed easily enough with Midas. He'd quickly finished every time they'd lain together and had been on his way almost before she was aware he'd released.

As Karnak escorted her back to her chamber, her body still glowed with energy from her orgasm and residual sparkles of delight like the facets of a gem catching the light. The problem was she'd allowed Svartan to shift the focus to giving her pleasure. She'd allowed him to take control, flip her onto her back and bring her to glorious fruition. Gwyneth would not make the same mistake again. Next time she would be the one in control even if she had to tie him to the bed to achieve it.

"Was your evening satisfactory, madam?" Karnak's pale eyes twinkled, creasing at the corners, and she wanted to slap the smile from his face.

Holding her head high, she adopted her most frosty, queenly tone. "Whether my evening was satisfactory or not is not your concern."

"Of course, madam." He paused then added, "I only ask because I care for your well being. It must be very difficult to be whisked away from all you know and brought to a strange place. But His Majesty is a good man and a wise and just king, although he does tend to possess a somewhat gloomy nature. I believe if you give him the opportunity to show his brighter side, you might find you are quite happy living here."

She didn't respond, although she listened intently.

Karnak strode alongside her for a few more paces before he resumed talking. "The master is rather like a gem in the rough. He simply wants for a little polishing to make him shine."

Again, Gwyneth mulled over what he'd said, but when she spoke, she changed the subject. "How is it that you speak the same language as we do above? I noticed the signs above the shops are written with foreign characters. Surely you have a native language."

"Naturally." Karnak released a rapid-fire spate of words that sounded like pebbles being flung at a granite wall. The language was rough and guttural and sounded angry. He resumed speaking in fluid tones. "We have had enough interaction with the topside world that we can speak your language fluently. Over many generations the upper class has practically adopted your language as its own. Only the lowest peasants speak only Elohimese.

"And here you are, madam. Delivered safely to your own room." He stopped in front of the sapphire studded door.

"Thank you."

Inside the room, Agnet was trying to calm a fussy Brea. She walked the child to and fro while humming a tune. Gwyneth was transfixed for a moment by the music, which was so different from any ballads or lullabies she knew. The rise and fall of the notes was exotic and foreign as if these underdwellers had invented an entirely different musical scale.

Agnet turned to her and smiled as she crooned to Brea, "Here's Mummy now, sweetness."

"Has she been crying long?" Gwyneth hastened across the room and took her child from the other woman. She felt ashamed and vile for surrendering to their captor and indulging in ecstasy while Brea cried for her. For those brief moments, every thought of her daughter, of everything, had flown from her mind. All the while she should have been concentrating solely on her goal of bringing Svartan to climax. What kind of a mother was she, what kind of a person?

"Not long. Don't worry. Babies cry and it doesn't hurt them one bit." Agnet smoothed Brea's fair hair with her pallid hand. "Trust me, I've several older children as well as my little one and not one of them has been ruined by having to wait for a meal."

Gwyneth loosened the front of her garment which she'd so recently laced and freed her breast.

"I've just changed her," Agnet added. "Is there anything else I can get for you, madam, before I bid you goodnight?"

"Is it night? How can you tell night from day down here?" Gwyneth sat in the chair near the bedside—fashioned of wrought iron, not wood, she noted—with the baby to her breast and looked up at the housekeeper. "There is so much I want to know about this place. Perhaps you can answer some of my questions."

Agnet paused, pursing her lips. "I can certainly understand your dismay at being torn away from all that's familiar and brought to a foreign world, and I will help you adjust whenever I can. But some of the answers you seek should only come from the master himself. You should ask him what you wish to know tomorrow. For now...well, it's been a momentous day for you. I suggest you rest. Goodnight, madam."

With that, she left the room.

Gwyneth was left alone in the silent room with only the quiet crackling of the fire on the hearth and Brea's sucking disturbing the silence. She gazed at her darling child and brushed a finger over her soft cheek. Brea reached out and grabbed it.

"I will do better next time, I promise," she swore. "A child can't live underground. I will free you from this place if it's the last thing I do."

When Gwyneth woke, she had no idea how long she'd slept or what time it might be. How could one tell in a windowless room with no sunlight streaming in to mark the hour of the day? Her body felt soft and pliant, comfortable and relaxed in a way she had not felt for a long time.

For the entire time of her pregnancy and following Brea's birth she'd been able to think of little but the impending doom threatening her child. That coupled with the added burden of keeping her horrible secret from her husband had worn her out. Her scouts had come and gone from her chamber secretly with their reports of finding no one to match her description of Svartan, and she had fretted and worried every day and night.

Honestly, it was a relief to have the worst come to pass at last, especially since the situation hadn't turned out nearly as badly as it might have. Brea hadn't been taken from her. They were still together. And there was still a chance for Gwyneth to win their freedom. She didn't feel nearly the sense of dread she'd felt when faced with a roomful of straw to spin into gold.

Whatever else he might be, Svartan was an honorable man...or demon. He would not go back on his word once he'd given it. She truly believed he would release them if she could fulfill her part of the bargain. And now, fully rested, Gwyneth felt more cheerful and confident that she could manage the task. The way he'd cried, "enough," and thrust her away from his cock last night was surely proof that she'd almost achieved her goal.

Next time, she would not be distracted. And in the mean time, she'd learn all she could about the world in which she'd landed. In case she didn't succeed in her mission, it was possible some little detail would supply the knowledge she needed to find another way out.

A soft gurgle came from the cradle. Brea had slept deeply, too, not waking Gwyneth for a night feeding for the first time since she'd been born. Gwyneth's breasts were hard and throbbing. She got Brea from her crib, changed her diaper, then sat in the chair and opened the front of her nightgown to allow the baby to nurse.

She sang a soft lullaby and cradled the infant. Her father's claim that Gwyneth was an incomparable singer was yet another of his fabrications, but she could carry a tune all right and she sang softly about fireflies and night birds flying on a summer evening.

A soft knock on the door stopped her song. She called out "Come in," expecting to see Agnet again, and froze when Svartan stood framed in the doorway. He was every bit as commanding and arresting as he'd appeared last night. The contrast between his white skin and raven hair was striking, and his magnetic eyes were fringed in soot-black lashes. Today he wore black breeches and waistcoat and polished black boots, no surprise, but his shirt was a deep wine-red.

For a moment, they both remained transfixed, Gwyneth staring at him, his gaze fixed on the baby at her breast. Then he walked slowly across the room toward them.

He made her nervous, towering over her. After the extreme intimacies they'd shared last night, how could she still feel so awkward around him? She would refuse to let him know he intimidated her. Gwyneth looked up—way up—to his face and saw he was looking at Brea. His eyes were wide and unguarded for the first time. An expression of...was it awe?...softened the harsh angles of his face.

Svartan reached out a hand as if he would touch Brea's wildly waving arm, but he pulled it back without touching her.

He stood watching for several more moments while Gwyneth's skin flushed pink. "She's very small," he finally said.

"Yes. She's a baby."

"I haven't been around them much. I didn't realize she would be so small."

Just then Brea's attention was finally dragged away from her prime objective—drinking as much as she could possibly hold—by the intrusion of Svartan's deep voice. She broke free of Gwyneth's nipple and stared at him, unblinking. What Gwyneth called her "wise owl" stare.

"Hello," the demon said.

Brea snorted and turned her attention back to eating.

"How often does she need to eat?"

"When she was first born, about every two hours. Less now." Gwyneth wondered if he even knew how old Brea was. He'd let five months slip by after her birth before sending an anonymous note announcing the date he would come to claim her. For that matter, how had he learned she even had a child? It was general knowledge throughout the kingdom, of course, but how did he get his information in his underground lair?

"Can you leave her long enough to take a tour of the house and grounds? Agnet would watch her." He paused then added, "Or we could take her with us."

"I would prefer to keep her with me. I'm not fond of nannies or nursemaids looking after my own daughter."

He dipped his head. "Very well. We shall go down to breakfast before beginning our tour. Perhaps later I could show you around the city as well."

Gwyneth boldly stripped her other breast bare and moved Brea to it, quite aware that Svartan was having a hard time keeping his gaze from her chest. Good. She would prepare him for round two throughout the day, teasing and taunting and flaunting her body at every opportunity. He would not best her again tonight.

She lifted her gaze to him again, one eyebrow lifted. “Would you kindly give me a moment to dress? I’m not prepared to go down to a meal.”

“Of course. I’ll, uh, wait for you outside.” Was that a slight falter she heard in his arrogant voice? He bowed and turned sharply to stride from the room, the militaristic precision of his turn somewhat ruined by his boot heel skidding on the floor.

Gwyneth smiled as the door closed behind him and she looked down at Brea. “This contest of wills is not over yet.”

Breakfast was as delicious a meal as dinner had been, although the spices and combination of foods was foreign to Gwyneth’s palate. She considered the ingenuity it must take to feed an entire population of people living underground and was quite impressed that they managed at all.

She regarded a strawberry as red as any she’d ever eaten. “What did your people eat before you started growing vegetables and fruit?”

“Fish, grubs and various kinds of lichens. Our diet was simple.” He sipped a glass of water but ate nothing. “We are not the same species as you. Our physiology is a little different and doesn’t require much sustenance, so we don’t eat nearly as often as topsiders do. But we do enjoy the flavors of more varied fare. I’ll admit I’m quite fond of peaches, myself. They taste like I imagine sunshine would feel.”

He smiled and Gwyneth’s heart beat faster at the harsh

beauty of his face.

"So, you've never felt sunlight? What happens if you're exposed to it?"

"The rays burn and blind, which is why Elohimese only go to the upper world at night." Svartan regarded his own pale hand. "Being a hybrid, I can lurk in shadowy woods at midday. I've seen the sun, but I certainly can't stand in an open field beneath it."

She looked at his long-fingered hand and a frisson of pleasure tickled her belly at the thought of what pleasure those fingers had given her last night. How odd to be sitting across from him now, chatting as if none of that had happened. And how strange to imagine a life lived in shadow and darkness, fearing the sun's rays.

She looked around the room, which was lit exactly as it had been the night before—no morning light streaming in the window to mark a new day. Only the presence of eggs to tell her this was breakfast and not dinner again. Did they have underground fowl, too?

Brea stirred on her lap, whimpering and flailing her arms. Gwyneth set aside her fork and shifted the baby to her shoulder, rubbing her back.

"Are you certain you won't have Agnet care for the child?"

"No, thank you. I can manage." She'd been through this before, Midas having made it clear to her how unqueenly it was for Gwyneth to go around the castle carrying the child in a sling that bound Brea to her.

Svartan nodded acknowledgment. "She is precious. I can understand why you don't wish to let her out of your sight."

Here was her opportunity. "And precious to you, too, evidently. You say you need an heir, but why my child? Why not any other baby in your kingdom? There must be thousands of your subjects who would be happy to give their child a better life by surrendering it into your care. Or orphans? Aren't there orphans you could adopt as your own?"

He didn't answer. His gaze dropped from hers as he rose from the table. "Come. We will walk now."

And with his refusal to answer, breakfast was over.

The tour of the house was brief. It was spacious and large, but no palace fit for a king. The furnishings were crafted of metal: iron, copper, gold or silver, and inlaid with gems that would've made Midas salivate with desire. But Gwyneth understood that down here the value of these polished metals and rocks was no greater than wood, marble or granite was in the world above. The silken cushions and carpets were probably worth more because the element from which they were crafted was rarer.

Without the sling to support her weight, Brea's sleeping body grew quite heavy. After a while, Gwyneth shifted the infant to her other arm.

Svartan stopped walking. Cocking his head, he studied them for a moment. "I will carry the child now." He didn't ask, didn't request. He announced.

Irritation swelled in Gwyneth at his confident tone. She stared at him challengingly, and he stared back.

He reached out his hands. "I will be careful. You must trust me."

Reluctantly, she handed Brea over. "Support her neck and her bottom. Hold her close, and for heaven's sake, don't drop her."

Svartan took the baby in his strong hands. "I can't decide whether you think of me as a bear or an imbecile."

Gwyneth glanced at him uncertainly. Though he didn't smile, she had the impression he was making a joke. Had there been jokes in those hot, mysterious nights of spinning? Sort of... She'd rather liked his deadpan humor before she'd discovered his callous trickery.

She opened her mouth to retort, but she realized he wasn't paying her any attention. His words had been distracted, almost without any thought at all. He was gazing down at Brea, who sighed and stirred, as if sensing the change of protective arms. Though he held her slightly awkwardly like any man unused to dealing with tiny infants, his grasp was sure yet gentle, his expression both wondering and curious. Like a scientist who'd discovered a particularly unusual specimen.

Without warning, his lips curved into a smile that lightened his eyes and his whole face. "I didn't realize a baby could be beautiful," he observed. "How can she be so tiny and yet look so much like you?"

Gwyneth blinked. "Was that a compliment?"

The smile disappeared. His dark lashes dropped like a protective veil. "To Brea," he said, and walked across the hall to the front door. A servant bowed them out of the house and closed the door behind them. "This way. I'll show you the new tribunal building first, since I have to go there anyway."

At first, he strode along too fast and she had to run to keep up with him. She wouldn't have bothered if he hadn't been carrying Brea. But as she trotted after him like some puppy, dodging among the pale, busy people to keep him in sight, indignation rose up like a tide. He was doing it deliberately to humiliate her, perhaps even to separate her from Brea.

He halted so unexpectedly that she ran into him. "Sorry," he said abruptly. "I'm used to walking alone." Thus depriving her of both anger and the perverse satisfaction of expressing it. She marched along beside him in silence, feeling grim and helpless. But at least at this slightly slower pace, she had the chance to take in her surroundings, the loose, cool garb of the pale city-dwellers who didn't as a rule wear the elaborate, layered clothing fashionable in her own world, even among the poor. Gwyneth supposed it was too hot down here. She began to feel her own gown, presumably designed to Svartan's specifications, made her stand out like a sore thumb. Certainly she was receiving plenty of stares, mostly curious, some downright stunned.

Of course, she was walking with their king, however unceremonious he appeared by Midas's standards. And that king was carrying her child in his arms.

"Do they know?" she blurted.

"Pardon?"

"Your people. Are they aware of your plans for my daughter?"

He hesitated. "Mostly no," he said at last. "I've discussed it with one or two of my closest advisers, of course—Karnak, for one, whom you met. But the majority of my people know nothing about you or Brea. I plan to introduce them to her formally one day. Perhaps on her first birthday, perhaps before."

He glanced at her. "We could discuss that. You'll know better than I when she can bear the noise and stress of cheering crowds."

Again, Gwyneth found herself catching her jaw in mid-dive. He seemed to have that effect on her. "You worry about cheering crowds when you've deprived her of fresh air?"

He frowned. "The air is perfectly fresh. In fact, it smells a lot sweeter than your city centre."

Reluctantly, Gwyneth was forced to concede that point. The air was a little over-warm, perhaps, but there was plenty of it and she could detect none of the unpleasant odors common in the crowded streets she was used to.

"How do you do that?" she asked curiously.

He shrugged. "Good ventilation. We have a system of ducts behind the rock that admits fresh air from above and filters out the old."

"That must have taken some work," she said, wonderingly, staring around her. It was a weird place, she thought, all irregular shapes and bizarre paths leading up and over buildings as well as around them. But it was ingenious in its own way, and oddly beautiful with the sparkling of precious minerals in among the hard granite. A tremendous feat of aesthetics as well as engineering.

"No," he said unexpectedly. "The planning was the hard part, but once we began it, the work was done really quickly. Everyone, from engineers to laborers, was eager to complete it."

She glanced at him. "You are responsible for this?" she asked, carefully neutral.

"I'm stubborn," said Svartan, adjusting his grip on the baby as she wriggled unexpectedly in his arm. "I insisted it could be done, and we found the way. Do you carry her with you like this all the time? Do you not have some sort of baby carriage?"

"Yes, for outdoors," Gwyneth answered, slightly thrown by the abrupt subject change. "She likes the motion. It soothes her when she's fractious."

He nodded. "I'll send someone to you this afternoon who will make one to your requirements. This is our daily market."

Distracted from her instinctive determination to decline his offer, Gwyneth found herself gazing around the colorful stalls which sold everything from jewelry to fish. Trinket boxes made of solid gold, studded with emeralds and sapphires, umpteen varieties of mushroom, bales of cloth of every conceivable color, working boots and sandals with one narrow strap to keep them on, belts and work bags, bright ribbons, jars and pots, glasses, vases, crockery of fantastic shapes and unusual sizes, tools, fruits Gwyneth had never seen before and some that she had.

"Most of the stuff you see is made here," he said, so casually that she knew he wanted her to notice. "Apart from the stall at the end which sells goods traded from topside. When I first became king, it was the other way 'round. One stall of our goods, twelve of theirs. Now we're learning what riches we have here."

He'd made a difference, she allowed with reluctance. He'd made life better for his people. "How long have you been king?" she asked.

He smiled faintly. "In name since I was sixteen. In practice, since I was twenty."

"You had some kind of regent until you came of age?"

"Not exactly. Bizarrely enough, although the kingdom is traditionally ruled by a harsh autocracy, the people may vote in the autocrat they prefer."

"An elective kingship?"

"Exactly. With the king chosen from one of the families within the royal blood line. I won when my grandfather died, but narrowly, since I had so much going against me—I'm a hybrid and I was only sixteen, and so people feared I would be controlled by unscrupulous men. I had to fight to keep my throne and to pacify rivals. And then I had to fight to keep down those aforementioned unscrupulous men who wanted to control me."

He spoke lightly and with wry humor, and yet Gwyneth glimpsed the grit and pain of those years before he'd won by sheer, steely determination, she suspected as much as by the brilliance which must even then have shone from him.

Shocked by the admiring direction of her thoughts, she let her gaze slide away from his and saw a lady tripping across from the market toward them. She was smiling, beautifully dressed in a midnight blue, loose robe that sparkled with diamonds. Gold rings flashed in her ears, on her wrists and ankles. Even her teeth sparkled. And from the fact that several servants followed her with arms full of purchases, Gwyneth suspected she was a noblewoman.

"Well met, Highness!" she said gaily, with a playful curtsy right in front of them. Svartan chose to halt. "Is that really a child you're clutching in your strong arms?"

"Yes," said Svartan, casting a quick glance at Brea which instantly softened his impatient face. "It does appear to be a child."

The woman, clearly oblivious to his sarcasm, said, "Goodness! Is it yours?"

Svartan's gaze fixed on her. Gwyneth held her breath. *Don't dare. Don't dare claim her...*

Yet why did she care what he said here? He'd already claimed her daughter as his heir. What difference did it make if this beautiful hell dweller believed that he was the father of Gwyneth's child?

But to her surprise, the woman began to blush and a look that was almost fear surged into her large, pale eyes. Of course. Everyone must know that hybrids couldn't breed, and the woman had just drawn his failing to his attention. No wonder she looked petrified. But at least Gwyneth was safe from her insult.

Insult? You are his mistress. He's done things to you your husband never came close to.

God, what did that make her?

It makes me a mother fighting for my child.

The woman gave an awkward laugh, but Svartan, as if he noticed nothing, said merely, "Lady Candara, Lady Gwyneth and her daughter. You must excuse us for the moment, Candara, I have an appointment."

Although Candara immediately stepped back with a smile, the glance she shot upward at Gwyneth was so piercing that it made her think. For some reason she didn't like the thought, and that made her angry enough to say waspishly, "Do I sense that Candara is one of those obliging ladies who ensure you don't degenerate into monkdom?"

Svartan didn't glance at her as they walked on down the rocky path toward a major building work at the very end. But a faint smile twisted his full lips. "On the contrary, Candara would hold out for marriage."

"Does she love you?" Gwyneth blurted. She tried to believe her tension was because this possibility could help her to freedom. But in this place, he was all she had, and her nature seemed to be perverse enough to turn it to jealousy.

"She'd love to be queen. Which is a pity since she never will be. What do you think of this building's shape? From this distance?"

Baffled by yet another change of subject, Gwyneth found herself regarding the new building at the end of the road. It was large, larger than Svartan's house and more classical in shape. Although built into the rocks, and its lines were straighter, its impression was one of space and grandeur. Despite the men on ropes and ladders swarming all over it, she realized this one was built to impress.

She considered. "I like it. It's different and yet still retains the distinctive quality of all your buildings."

He smiled at her answer. Sensing it, she met his gaze and saw with surprise that her words had really mattered to him. He wanted her approval. Perhaps just because she was of the other world. And a queen to boot, God help her.

He walked on in silence. As they drew nearer to the building, a familiar figure bounded forward to greet them.

"We meet again," beamed Karnak, in bright purple today. Now that she was in a better condition to notice such things, though, she realized his suit was of light silk, and that his trousers were loose and comfortable looking, in all far more suitable for down here than the tight breeches and heavy velvet coats of her own world.

In fact, it struck her that they were probably more suitable for a summer's day above ground, too, but court etiquette would never stretch that far. In her own layered gown, despite the fine material, she'd begun to feel unappealingly sweaty.

Karnak was examining the baby in Svartan's arms. "What a beautiful infant," he exclaimed. "Look at his skin..."

"Her skin," said Svartan and Gwyneth in unison. Karnak glanced quizzically from one to the other until Svartan cleared his throat and turned hastily to Gwyneth, offering Brea to her.

"Does she need to be changed?" Gwyneth asked in surprise.

"I've no idea," Svartan confessed. "But I can't take her into the building site. Wait here with Karnak. I won't be long."

Stunned by his thoughtfulness, Gwyneth took Brea and watched him stride across to the main building. Several men converged to meet him.

Realizing that Karnak's perceptive, pale eyes were on her face, Gwyneth said brightly, "So this is his tribunal building? What's it for?"

"Tribunal meetings. A bit of government administration."

"What does the tribunal do? What is it?"

Karnak considered. "We're still finding out. It's a very new idea to us, an institution for the discussion and passing of laws in conjunction with the king, a place to debate and initiate changes in government. The people vote in representatives to speak for them."

"Like a parliament?" Gwyneth said, enlightened. "But Svartan said the king was an autocrat."

"Our kings were, until Svartan," Karnak said drily, and when he'd caught her eye to his satisfaction he added, "Svartan has a vision beyond what we lesser beings can imagine. Yet he makes things happen, and we like them. There's opposition to this, too, but he believes it will stop the sort of faction fighting that surrounded his own succession, make for continuity and a smoother transfer of power."

"Will it?" Gwyneth said faintly.

"I expect so, knowing Svartan." His gaze dropped to the sleeping Brea. "Especially if his successor follows his lead."

"So that's why he..." She broke off, but really, there was no need. Karnak seemed to be aware of just about every nuance surrounding her kidnap to this place.

And Karnak himself was clearly not one to beat about the bush. "Wants an heir. Yes," he said emphatically. "For all his improvements, in fact. There are those who'd like a return to the old ways, which let a few greedy families feather their own nests, and those of a few of their cronies."

Gwyneth found herself nodding slowly. Svartan was already striding back toward them.

Karnak said, "I've just been explaining your tribunal fantasy to your lady."

"Ignore him," Svartan advised. "Karnak believes in it as much as I do. Dinner tonight," he added severely to the grinning man in purple.

"How could I refuse so gracious an invitation?"

"And Karnak?"

"Highness?"

"Change your clothes first."

Karnak laughed and went on his way.

"So," Svartan murmured, taking Brea back from Gwyneth without a word of permission. It spoke volumes that the infant didn't protest being held by a strange man. "What do you think of tribunals? Do you believe it will work?"

"I believe it does, in some countries."

"Does it in yours?"

"We don't really have one. Midas has a council of sorts, but it just approves everything he proclaims."

"Then who speaks for the people?" he demanded.

"No one. Unless they have a benevolent lord."

He nodded thoughtfully. "That's the impression I got. Are the people happy?"

"Most of them...not really. And yet it doesn't take much to improve their lives..."

She found herself telling him of the minor changes she'd managed to make in her months as queen, and the differences it had made to the hard lives of so many. But it didn't bear comparison with his huge endeavors, and she hastily said so.

However, when she dared to meet them, his eyes didn't condemn her. In fact, they were unexpectedly warm. "You must tell me," he said, "if anything strikes you about my kingdom. It is too easy to lose perspective, and I would value your thoughts."

"You would?" She scanned his expression for evidence of mockery but found none.

"I would." A smile flickered and was gone. "Is that so hard to believe? Did Midas not admire your reforming zeal?"

"Actually," she said in a rush, "I found it best that he didn't know. He is not...a man of the people."

"Am I? Hybrid and tradition-wrecker as I am?"

"I don't know," she said honestly. Then, "In the sense that you care for your people, yes you are." And that was the truth. His difference, his arrogant belief that he was right and his opponents wrong, didn't matter beside that one all-important fact. He deserved to be king. Even she could see that.

What he didn't deserve was to bury Brea and herself underground for the rest of their lives, even if he did offer Brea all the royal power which Midas would never bestow on his daughter, a mere female.

Chapter Twelve

Although she was loath to admit it, Gwyneth's day was unexpectedly fascinating. As well as glimpses into Svartan's profound and tortured mind, she was granted a new view of his strange but far from unlovely country. She was shown local beauty spots that yesterday would have appalled her, yet today, through his eyes and his people's, she could see they had indeed their own weird and spectacular beauty.

In the afternoon, he returned her to his palace and went off without explanation. After she'd fed and changed Brea, she was served lunch, during which Agnet asked permission to bring in her own children, and the two women watched them play. Agnet's older children were good with the babies, and particularly careful with Brea, so Gwyneth's anxiety soon faded into comfort.

Only as the dinner hour again approached did her nervousness resurface. Svartan had given her no clue as to when he would choose his next night of sexual torture, but it was clear from last night that he liked to surprise her. He might just do it again by declaring for tonight. Whichever night he chose, she had to be ready.

And so, in privacy, while Brea lay on her bed and gurgled and played with a borrowed rattle, she tore her old petticoat up into strong, thick strips, and thought carefully about their next encounter. There was no way she'd give up control this time.

However, planning her moves in detail made her uncomfortably hot. Her body couldn't forget the pleasure he'd induced in her before, and the thought of having his naked body at her command couldn't but arouse her. She had to speak to herself sternly as she changed her gown for dinner, because if she couldn't control her body in his absence, she didn't have much chance in his very physical, naked presence. Oh, but she could so easily imagine sliding onto his long, hard cock...

Stop! It's he who's to come, not you!

She actually jumped when the knock sounded on her door. Fearing Svartan himself, she smoothed down her hair and held her head high before giving a casual instruction to enter.

It was merely Agnet, however, and with a servant, not even Karnak this time, to conduct her to the dining room. As if she couldn't remember where to find it. Every room, every passage of this house that she'd ever been in or glimpsed, was etched in her memory.

Her heart hammered as she followed the servant down stone steps and corridors. Tonight's dinner was likely to be even more of a trial than last night's since she was to face company as well as Svartan, and she had no idea how he would behave toward her, whether he would command her to his chamber in their presence or not.

The servant threw open the dining room door, and Gwyneth was treated to the rare sight of Svartan laughing out loud, his head thrown back in unrestrained humor. Something turned over in her stomach, an ache, an unspecific longing she had no name for. But as she entered the room, Svartan, Karnak and a woman turned toward her, and the laughter died in Svartan's face.

He came toward her, civilly bowing as he had last night and introduced her to the Karnak's wife, who was called Guzel. As plump and calm as her husband was thin and lively, Guzel had friendly, intelligent eyes and a mouth full of perceptive questions that narrowly avoided vulgar nosiness. Gwyneth gave her the benefit of the doubt because, like Karnak, Guzel made her laugh. In fact, the evening flew by in witty and entertaining conversation that encompassed many subjects to which she could contribute, including the literature of her own land.

"You have such books here?" she said once in surprise.

"Many," said Karnak, amused. "In fact, right..."

"We have yet to know many things about each other," Svartan interrupted, and when her gaze connected with his, he added softly, "Have we not?"

Heat flushed through her. His meaning was obvious, and what was worse, its significance was unlikely to be lost on Guzel or Karnak.

"Clearly," she said coldly. Svartan sat back in his chair, regarding her with a faint smile on his mocking, predatory lips. His mood appeared to have swung, or perhaps he'd just stopped pretending to be the genial host. Either way, for all his face gave away, he might as well still have worn the cowled hood.

"Let's change that," he suggested. "Ask me anything you want to know."

His provoking gaze and taunting voice both challenged her to ask what she really wanted to know. *What will make you come?*

Well, that was one game she wouldn't play in public.

"What I want to know right now," she said evenly, "is when it would be polite to retire for the night. I'm very tired, and my daughter is likely to wake soon."

From the corner of her eyes, she saw Guzel's eyebrows fly up in her husband's direction. Svartan's expression, however, remained impassive. Only the faintest tightening of one finger around the stem of his glass gave away that her words might have bothered him.

He pushed the glass away and stood in one abrupt yet fluid movement.

"Whenever you wish. I shall escort you."

"That won't be necessary," she said in sudden panic.

"Nevertheless," said Svartan, striding to the door.

"Is the party over?" said Karnak brightly. "Good night, my lady, Highness..."

Gwyneth barely managed a civil goodnight to the couple she had come to like before she swept past Svartan and out the door into the stone passage. Looking neither to right nor left, she sailed ahead of him with her head held high and her most forbidding expression plastered to her face. It hid the deep sense of panic rising up from her toes to consume her.

He was going to choose tonight. His teasing guaranteed it. The fact that he came with her removed all doubt. She could do no more than make it plain she didn't want their tryst to be tonight and hope her aversion put him off. Despite her vague thoughts and plans, she truly wasn't ready for this. And yet a traitorous trickle of excitement was seeping from her pussy. The image of his finely toned, pale, naked body danced before her eyes.

She walked even faster, and yet by the time she reached her bedchamber door, he was right beside her.

Taking a deep breath for courage, she glared at him. "It seems I have to point out to you that I will not indulge in any sexual congress in front of my daughter. Our business will not be contracted in this chamber."

He inclined his head. "As you wish."

Once again, her sails were deprived of wind. An instant longer, she hesitated, waiting for him to command her to his chamber instead. Then she laid her hand on the door latch.

"I have a request," said Svartan.

Her eyes closed. *This is it. Fetch the bindings and dredge your imagination. You could be out of here by morning.*

"Very well," she said as steadily as she could.

"Gwyneth," he reproved, his voice unexpectedly soft. "Have you learned nothing from me yet? You haven't even heard my request and yet you're agreeing to it. Again."

"I agreed to it last night," she whispered. And angry, frightened and uncertain as she was, she couldn't prevent the upsurge of excitement that tightened her nipples and danced in her stomach.

He said, "You agreed to a deal last night. This is a request which you are at perfect liberty to reject."

She turned her surprised gaze up to his face, searching his eyes. "You're mocking me."

"No." He stirred. "That is, I was teasing you a little, downstairs, just to see what you would do. I have my answer to that. I just want to ask you..." He took a quick breath. "...if I might say goodnight to Brea."

Gwyneth closed her lips. Her refusal was already forming there, and yet some half-embarrassed seriousness in his face kept the words at bay. He wanted this. It was nothing to do with Gwyneth or with dominance games. It was about Brea.

"Very well," she said abruptly and, lifting the latch, she strode into the room.

Agnet arose from the nursing chair with alacrity, coming swiftly toward them. "She's still asleep," she murmured. "Good as gold."

"Thank you, Agnet."

Agnet bobbed a curtsey and a smile at them both and

departed. God knew what she thought of her king being here.

Gwyneth stood by the cradle, regarding her sleeping daughter. Milk began to drip from her aching breasts. Although she didn't hear him move, Svartan appeared at the other side of the cradle. Slowly, Gwyneth lifted her gaze from the baby to her captor.

As before, there was a faint smile on his lips, a softened expression in his eyes as he watched the child sleep. He reached out his hand and, lighter than a butterfly wing, he brushed one finger against her soft, silken cheek. His smile quirked and he withdrew his hand.

Already, he'd shown Brea more affection than Midas had since her birth. Without warning, he glanced up and caught her staring. For an instant, neither moved. Then Brea heaved a huge sigh that shook her entire body and she yawned and stretched. Her face began to crumple, emitting a couple of small whimpers that were the prelude to full scale yelling.

"What's the matter with her?" Svartan asked in alarm.

Gwyneth laughed. "She's hungry." She bent and lifted her, which staved off the bellow, though only for an instant.

"So you'll feed her and then retire? Will she sleep till morning?"

"Yes. And I hope so."

Svartan nodded. "Is there anything you need? A drink, perhaps?"

She glanced at the glass and jug of water by the nursing chair. "Thank you. But it seems Agnet thinks of everything."

"Of course," he said, turning away. "Good night."

Gwyneth almost called him back, though why and for what she didn't know. In any case, the impatience of the baby distracted her, and by the time he shut the door, she was already seated in the chair with the baby firmly latched to her breast. But she found herself gazing at the closed door in baffled wonder. For some reason, she felt ridiculously touched.

Ragnorak returned to the dining room in the expectation of having it to himself to get drunk in. However, Karnak sat at the table once more, swirling wine around his glass. Ragnorak poured himself a fresh one and knocked it back, after which he refilled the glass and began to pace the room.

"I see," said Karnak.

"What do you see?" Ragnorak flung over his shoulder.

"I see you haven't a clue what you're doing with that girl."

"I know exactly what I'm doing with that girl. Who, incidentally, was once queen of her own world and will one day be queen of mine."

There was a short silence. Then Karnak said flatly, "Not if you bewilder her with your ill-natured mood swings or treat her courtship as if it was one of your wretched games."

Ragnorak threw himself into a chair and forced his head back against the emerald-seamed wall with an audible thump. "It's how I began it. It's how I have to finish it."

"Will it be worth it to have the child now if you don't have the mother?"

Ragnorak let the smile twist his lips. "There's the rub, my friend. I can't have one without the other. I've made another deal and I may have to let them both go. Or live with her in the hell of never touching her. Would that be worse? To avoid it, I have to win her as well as the bet."

He regarded his old friend for a few moments, then drank the rest of his wine and set down the glass. "I don't stand a chance, do I?"

Karnak gave a lopsided smile. "Oh, I don't know. You

fascinate her and infuriate her. Perhaps that's a beginning. Certainly, she's not indifferent to you. If you want my opinion of her—and in fact, even if you don't—I think she's a strong, honest, passionate and fun woman who is worthy of rather more than abduction and tricky deals."

"I know it. I've always known it. I'm too...driven. I need to make it right."

"There is one other slight impediment. Your queen is already married to a different king."

"She divorced him."

Karnak blinked. "Did you force her to do that too?"

"Oh, no. She knows she should never have married him. He's a greedy, materialistic and utterly self-centered moron." He lifted his wine glass and thrust it commandingly in Karnak's direction. "He is also, of course, my loving half-brother."

Chapter Thirteen

It was the strangest week of Gwyneth's life. It began to feel almost natural to wake up and go to sleep in the same evenly lit darkness, to eat the strange if often delicious underworld food and walk among the white-skinned denizens of hell as if they were normal people.

She no longer thought of them as demons. Not even her abductor, who displayed such wildly contradictory character traits. She never quite knew when she would see him. He would take odd moments from his hectically full schedule just to watch Brea play, or to take them both to see something he'd thought might entertain them. And yet the evening meals, from which she was never excused, whether they were alone as on that first evening or in company, he deliberately infused with sexual tension.

She learned to deal with it, smiling innocently or popping food into her mouth with a suggestive deliberation that made him shift in his seat. He didn't hold all the cards. He wanted her. That was clear from the bulge in his pants that he couldn't always hide. And yet the week passed with no summons to his chamber.

Instead, leaving Brea with Agnet and her children for an hour, he took her clambering over rocks and streams. Away from the city, she felt able to remove her shoes and stockings and hitch up her skirts to leap around as she hadn't since childhood. Svartan, agile as a mountain goat, led the way, diving through waterfalls, jumping over streams and sliding across slippery rocks. It was gloriously childish, and Gwyneth heard herself laughing almost with surprise. When had she last had fun?

The thought distracted her, and she missed her footing when she jumped. Her arms flailed, her feet struggled to grip the rock, and she fell.

Svartan leapt back to catch her, breaking her fall with his own, and yet somehow as they rolled, she ended up underneath him, gazing breathlessly up into his fascinating face. His eyes were so dark, glimmering lights of lust flickering with the reflected stream. Gwyneth's stomach turned over. Her heart beat fast like a bird's. Svartan's weight was heavy on her, but curiously sweet and dangerously exciting. Between her sprawled legs, she could feel the outline of his cock growing.

For several moments they lay perfectly still. Then he broke her gaze, glancing lower to her lips and cheeks, her throat and breasts. Taking more of his weight on one elbow, he slowly lifted his hand and placed it over her left breast.

Hot pleasure shot through to her fingertips, to her womb. Her nipple rose up to greet his palm and he began to rub it very slowly, very gently. Each tiny movement caused exquisite sparks that caught at her breath. His gaze came back to hers, watching her reaction and she, too stunned or too amazed to move, stared back. She knew it should be a repelling stare, but somehow she doubted it. His hand felt too good on her breast, the hard ridge of his cock against her pulsing pussy just too wonderful to reject.

Deliberately, he slid his hand inside the neck of her gown and began again on her naked skin, using just his palm to rub her nipple, oh-so-lightly flicking across it, over and over.

She opened her trembling mouth to say something,

anything to break the spell of desire under which she was so rapidly sinking, but she never did. For he simply lowered his head and took her mouth, matching the rhythm of his kiss to the movement of his devastating hand.

Gwyneth arched into him without meaning to. Very slowly, very lightly, he began to rub his cock against her while he kissed her and caressed her breast. The sound of the waterfall and the rushing stream filled her ears. The sweet, earthy smells of fresh water overlaid the warm, distinctive scents she always associated with Svartan. It was like a taught reaction. One hint of him and her whole body seemed to salivate.

The kiss broke naturally. A very faint smile played about his lips and eyes, but still he said nothing. Softly, he took his hand from her breast and eased his weight off her before getting to his feet and holding out his hand to help her rise.

Bemused, Gwyneth gave her own. She wondered if she was being taken to a cave, to some other suitable place where he would claim his second two hours.

Oh, no, he can't, she thought in panic. I haven't got what I need!

But he claimed nothing, merely carried on jumping over rocks, back the way they'd come until they rediscovered their stockings and shoes. Then he asked her thoughts on his tribunal and listened carefully to her opinions before taking her back to the palace and leaving her.

But that evening, they dined alone. Gwyneth could hardly eat because of the strength and speed of her heartbeat. She was sure it would be tonight, and she welcomed it with more than a simple desire for freedom. She was ready for him now and to gain her daughter's freedom, surely she was allowed a little wicked sexual pleasure of her own.

When the meal was done, he rose and laid her trembling hand on his arm and conducted her to her own bedchamber, where, as usual, he touched Brea's cheek by way of a goodnight caress. After which, he merely kissed Gwyneth's hand and departed.

Leaving her a mass of confused and tangled emotions that tore her apart.

Ragnorak was winning. He sensed it. Her body still craved him, more powerfully than ever. And she could see he was no demon, that he worked hard for his people, and she admired that in him. More than those things, he'd seen her eyes light up with rather more than challenge when he came upon her unexpectedly. And yesterday's kiss, with no sexual favor asked or expected, had done his cause no harm at all.

With this in mind, he hurtled through his self-assigned early morning tasks and strode impatiently to her bedchamber. He would offer to end their deal and instead offer her marriage, half of his kingdom, and the whole of his heart, which had always been hers from the first kiss in a room full of golden threads.

He rapped once on her bedchamber door but didn't trouble to listen for the reply before entering.

She didn't hear him. She was standing almost up against the opposite wall. Her body shook. She held Brea over one shoulder, as if winding her, and the baby grinned at him with recognition. His heart turned over before Gwyneth heard his footfalls and spun round in alarm. And he saw why she shook.

Her whole body was racked with huge, silent sobs. The evidence ran down her cheeks, into her hair and her mouth and dripped on to her neck and the hands that held her daughter.

Stricken, he stared at her.

She whispered, "There are no windows. No doors to the outside. No sky, no sun. Svartan, we are dying here..."

He couldn't bear it. He swung around and left, leaning against the closed door. So near and yet so far. He'd known she would grieve for her own world, but he hadn't expected it to affect him so profoundly.

It was natural. But she wasn't dying. The baby was even smiling. And Gwyneth wasn't truly unhappy. He could swear she'd enjoyed yesterday. She was merely homesick. And maybe there was something he could do to alleviate that.

Straightening, he opened the door and found her pacing the room with Brea falling asleep on her shoulder. Her face was dry now, if still somewhat streaky as she stared at him with defiance.

"Come with me," he said gently, and she was so surprised, she went without a murmur.

He took her to his library, his most prized possession because it contained the best books he knew from both their cultures.

"Look," he said, pulling a large book on botany from the shelf and opening it at the picture plates showing various woodland flowers. "On this side are all books in your own language. Art, science, literature. You're welcome to read them whenever you wish."

She swallowed, gazing from the books to his face, then back to the large, leather-bound botany volume. As if she couldn't help it, she took one hand from Brea's back and touched the painted flower with her fingertips.

"I didn't show you them before because I thought they would just feed your homesickness," he admitted. "But maybe they can help, instead."

She frowned, staring at him. "You think books are a *substitute*? The only help you can give me is to let us go free."

Every word was like a dagger in his heart. He laughed at

himself for the easy victory he'd been imagining only minutes ago. She wasn't won. She was nowhere near won.

He said quietly, "That wasn't the deal." And turning away, he left her with the books.

Midas stared into the strained and wizened face of the man pilloried with cuffs on his hands and feet. He could tell by the vacant stare in the old fool's eyes that they'd gleaned all the useful information they could from him. His addled, decrepit brain would give no more details about Midas's father and the lusty love of his youth no matter how much he was tortured.

Heaving an exasperated sigh, Midas stepped back and folded his arms across his chest. "Very well. Let him go."

"Do you mean let him go from the castle or from the stocks? Should I have him returned to the dungeon to await further questioning?" Wallace was a stickler for precise directions.

"I mean let him go. As in, take him back to whatever alley you found him scavenging in. He doesn't know any more than anyone else about my long lost brother." *Or his ridiculous name!*

"What I need is to start thinking about this in a more creative way." Midas found his steward was an excellent listener. He never interrupted and he always agreed. It helped the king to air his thoughts aloud to his most toadying confidant.

"What I need is to stop trying to find old timers who know nothing and seek a denizen of this so-called underworld who might help me find out some news about Gwyneth. I may never remember or learn my half-brother's name, but that doesn't mean I can't find another way to achieve my goal."

"Absolutely, sir." Wallace bobbed his head and motioned for the guards to unfasten the old man attached to the pillory.

When they did, he slumped into a pile on the floor, looking like nothing so much as a heap of rags. A pair of guards lifted and carried the man from the dungeon chamber.

Midas continued. “Send out soldiers, spies and servants to search the length and breadth of the land for any creature that even hints of being a denizen of the underworld. Goblins, elves, demons or mere men—whatever these creatures are—I want at least one brought here for questioning. Do you understand?”

“Yes, Your Highness.”

“As extra incentive, I will give a purse of gold to the first man who brings me a specimen. And Wallace?”

“Yes, sire?”

“As extra incentive for you personally, if you mobilize this search party and bring me such a person within the week, I will *not* fire you and give your job to someone younger and cleverer. How does that sound?”

“Very generous, Highness. Thank you.” The steward bowed his way out of the chamber, leaving Midas alone.

He stared at the blood-streaked pillory, wondering what it might feel like to have one’s head, hands and feet immobilized while someone flailed one’s back raw or punched the stupid, obsequious smile off one’s face. Very painful, no doubt.

But one couldn’t squeeze blood from a potato and clearly he’d been questioning the wrong sort of people. By focusing his search in a new direction, surely he’d finally get the results he needed.

And then he would reclaim his bloody bride and his baby, too, even if he had to take his army and storm the underworld to get them.

Chapter Fourteen

"You're a very powerful man. I'm not denying that. You can command the elements, turn straw into gold and cause rocks to split apart and come back together again. All I'm saying is that in certain circumstances you're not as strong as you think you are. There are some things even you can't handle."

"I can deal with one tiny baby for a couple of hours." Svartan bent over Brea's crib like a big, looming gargoyle and let her cling to his finger.

"No. I really don't think you can. Not when Brea starts screaming. She can make your ears bleed, and you have no breast with which to appease her." Gwyneth folded the clean white diaper in her hands.

"But you're not afraid to leave her with Agnet."

"Agnet is a mother. She knows what to do."

"I could learn if you'd let me."

"Now you're just pouting, which is so unattractive." Gwyneth hid her smile. When had their relationship changed from captor and captive to this light, amusing banter? And exactly how many days had passed since she and Brea had come down here? It was easy to lose track.

He straightened, scowling. "Fine. You go have your luncheon with the ladies and leave Agnet in charge. It's not as if I have no work of my own to tend to."

"You work too hard." She tossed the diaper down and crossed to him, resting a hand on his arm. "You should think about taking some time for yourself. Or for me."

Her intent might be obvious, but she was tired of waiting for him to demand his second trial with her. She was tired of being underground, no matter how lavish the accommodations or how kind her host or how amenable all the people she'd met so far had been. Did he plan to wait until the very last two days of their allotted month to finish this? Well, she didn't have the patience to wait any longer.

"What if instead of my going to lunch with Lady Candara, I spent those same hours with you?" She slid her hand along his bare, muscular forearm. "I think it would be much more enjoyable for us both. I have some things I'd like to try..." She trailed off, leaving him with the suggestion that those "things" were the most erotic, taboo, sensual acts he could imagine.

His tongue darted out to flick over his lips. "You want our next session to be now?"

"If you don't feel you're ready, we can wait." She shrugged, letting him know she doubted his ability to hold out this time, no matter how much preparation time she gave him. She moved in close, her body mere inches away from his and his heat radiating through her lightweight garment. Nudging against the bulge in his breeches, she whispered, "I wouldn't want you to give in *too* easily."

"Madam, you think too highly of your charms. I assure you, whatever wiles you have in mind, I can withstand them."

Gwyneth nodded. "Then let's retire to your chamber and find out."

"Very well." He met her gaze with a challenging stare of his own intended to make her uncomfortable. But she knew him better now. He couldn't shake her confidence if she didn't let him.

Besides, she was armed with tools this time. She went to the dresser drawer where she'd hidden the lengths of torn petticoat beneath some undergarments.

He watched her as she placed the makeshift ropes in a bag. And Gwyneth watched him from the corners of her eyes, gauging his reaction. If he was impressed by her ingenuity in crafting the ropes or aroused by the idea of bondage, he didn't show it.

Agnet arrived to take over Brea's care. When they left the room, Brea was in her arms, reaching for a sparkling mirror-studded rattle which Agnet held just out of reach. Gwyneth decided that was how she must treat Svartan today. She would tease and torture him as he had her, bringing him close to climax again and again until the merest brush of a feather would put him over the edge.

Her body burned and shivered at the same time, and she was grateful she wasn't the one who had to hold out from orgasm. Her pussy was already melting like wax, moisture trickling down her thighs at the mere thought of Svartan in chains—or homemade bonds, as the case may be.

His room, which she hadn't seen since the night of her failure, was as she remembered it, dimly lit, very masculine, with spare yet well-appointed furnishings. The bed was a world away from Midas's pillow-laden, overly soft bed. The four posts were carved stone, a deep black that shimmered with elusive iridescent greens and purples.

The white coverlet had been replaced by one of deep purple. She pulled it back to reveal equally dark plum-colored sheets beneath. She began to tie her little ropes to the posts, tossing a casual, "You may undress and lie down now," to Svartan.

Gwyneth snuck a glance at him to see if he obeyed, and her already pattering heart beat faster at the sight of him removing his shirt at her command. His head was bent as he unfastened the buttons and a fringe of his black hair fell over his forehead, curtaining his eyes. Her fingers itched to brush it back, to feel those silky strands between her fingers and then to stroke her hand down the side of his face.

She turned her attention back to knot-tying. Of course, he would be able to break her braided bonds easily enough, if he truly desired, but it was the idea of shackling that counted.

"How do you want me? Face up or down?" His deep voice sent a renewed shiver vibrating through her. His words may be submissive, but the tenor of his voice would always sound commanding.

Although she'd had these days—weeks?—to plan her strategy, his question took her by surprise. She'd assumed face up. That was the side his cock was on. What could a woman do with a man's backside? She tried to imagine, and the intriguing ideas that occurred sent a wave of heat shimmering through her.

"You may lie on your back," she informed him coolly as if he hadn't thrown her at all. "But first, I will blindfold you." She held up the black silk scarf with which he'd once blindfolded her, the scarf she'd kept hidden after their encounter in the midst of piles of gold. If he was surprised to see she still had it, Svartan didn't show it.

Gwyneth remembered the night she'd worn the scarf as he examined her nude body and touched her all over. She'd felt vulnerable, stripped bare, yet powerful at the same time for she'd realized how her body enflamed him by the ragged sound of his breathing and his quiet groans. Now it was her turn to wield the power of the blindfold, cutting off Svartan's sight the better to enhance his other senses.

Svartan turned around, bending his knees slightly so she could reach high enough to tie the fabric around his head. After it was fastened, she led him to the bed, although he probably could've found his way there blind. He sat on the edge, then reclined on his back.

Gwyneth gazed at the contrast between his pale body and the deep purple sheets. He was aggressively masculine with his broad shoulders and long legs, his chiseled chest and big hands. But soon he would be spread-eagle and helpless. Her heart beat faster as she imagined it. She loved the idea of having this strong, commanding man at her disposal.

But enough imagining. She'd done nothing but for days. Now it was time to make the image a reality. Moving to the head of the bed, she grasped his wrist and drew his arm high. She tied his wrist to the piece of rope she'd already fastened to the bed so his arm was pulled straight. How nice that he had such a large bed to allow her to position him exactly the way she wanted.

She did the same on the opposite side before stepping back to admire the effect of his arms stretched over his head and bound tight. Moving to the foot, she bound his left ankle and right, pulling his legs apart and leaving him in an X across the bed. The sinews of his arms and legs were beautifully delineated. His cock stood erect from its thatch of dark hair, the heavy sac of his balls drawn tight beneath. He was certainly aroused.

Gwyenth studied every aspect of his body: the dark hair that sprinkled his abdomen and legs and tufted in his armpits, the hard planes of his jaw and chin and jutting nose below the black sash that covered his eyes, the flat discs of his areolae with the tiny buds of nipples. She left him waiting, anticipating her first touch, for she'd learned from experience that expectation was a large part of the game.

His lips parted and he exhaled. His fingers curled and clenched, and the long muscles of his arms rippled. Svartan shifted, checking the limits of his movement in this spread-eagle position, and Gwyneth smiled at the control she had over him. Let him try to get through the next couple of hours without coming.

She moved toward the bed, leaned over him and licked lightly over his right nipple. His senses were so heightened, he gasped as if she'd burned him with a brand. Gwyneth lightly nipped the taut bud, and his back arched off the bed. His reaction to her touch worked magic in her own body. Her nipples tingled, and her milk threatened to let down even though she'd so recently nursed Brea. And the fire between her legs...she didn't even want to think about. Best to concentrate on the task at hand.

After she'd kissed and licked one nipple, she moved to the other side. He would be expecting the same treatment, little licks and nibbles, and so she gave him something totally different. She pinched his nipple hard, twisted it almost viciously. He hissed and bucked beneath her punishing fingers. She let go, replacing fingers with mouth and soothing him with soft licks.

Meanwhile, she scraped her fingernails down his stomach, clawing lightly all the way from chest to groin. The base of her palm bumped against his cock. She scratched the length of his shaft, and this time it was his hips rising off the bed, as far as they could with his legs bound.

Gwyneth retreated, leaving him to dwell on the sensation. She stood and moved to the foot of the bed, watching him as his chest moved up and down from his rapid breathing and his fingers curled and uncurled. His cock was quivering, and she wondered if he might come without her even stimulating it directly.

She brushed her fingertips from the soles of his feet to his toes. He jerked, pulling against his bonds. The homemade ropes stretched, but were braided tightly enough that they didn't give.

Gwyneth climbed on the bed between his spread legs and lowered her head. She swept her hair up the length of one of his legs, allowing the ends to tickle his flesh from ankle to thigh. Poor Svartan groaned.

She draped her hair over his cock, feathering his erection with swishes of the silky strands. And she did the same to his balls, teasing them with gentle playfulness. But pleasure was best balanced by a little pain, so she soon abandoned her friendly torture to try something a little rougher.

Again Gwyneth rose from the bed. She moved toward the top and leaned over to kiss Svartan's mouth. His head rose from the pillow as he sought a deeper kiss, his tongue searching between her lips to find hers. She pulled away, leaving him reaching in vain and she went to the fire pit where hot coals burned red.

Candles were in short supply down here since the lighting was mostly from the strange crystals or oil lanterns, but Gwyneth had asked Agnet to get her a few, claiming the candle glow made her feel more at home. She drew the four-inch stub of a taper from her pocket, quickly stripped off her gown, then lit the candle from the coals on the hearth.

She watched the pretty yellow flame dance then grow steady. Wax melted, beading and rolling down toward her fingers. When the wax touched them, it barely stung. Gwyneth had secretly played with wax in her chamber, so she knew it would be just painful enough but not excruciating for Svartan.

Returning to the bed, she passed the candle over his chest close enough that he could feel the heat, but without spilling any wax on him...yet. His nostrils flared as he inhaled the waxy scent of the candle and understood what she was about to do.

"Just don't singe the hair off my balls, please," he murmured with a little smile.

"I wouldn't dream of harming you more than you would

enjoy." She tipped the candle just a bit, and a thin drizzle of wax splashed onto his chest just above his left nipple.

Svartan gritted his teeth and frowned—or at least she thought he did. It was hard to tell, as that part of his face was hidden by the scarf. He set his jaw tight, steeling himself for her next assault.

Gwyneth watched the wax harden to a paler red. It made pretty patterns on his white skin. She drizzled a line below his breast bone down toward his belly, and it flowed toward either side of his body before hardening. Svartan let out a low groan that time.

She moved lower. Would wax on his penis be too much? Was the flesh too sensitive? The purpose of this experiment was his arousal. She didn't want to hurt him to the point where she couldn't fuck him after a bit.

"Tell me if this stings too much," she whispered, and then she tipped the candle again letting only a single fat drop land on his shaft. But it slid all the way down to the base, leaving a sizzling trail.

Svartan cursed in his native tongue. At least she assumed he was cursing, but as rough as the language sounded he could have been praising her technique and begging for more. Gwyneth decided to err on the side of caution and abandoned the genital area. She moved farther down and splashed a little wax on his thighs, earning another exciting twist and curse from him. But the fast burning candle was already growing too short, too close to her hand so she ended the game by blowing it out.

"Poor thing. Does it hurt much?" she asked as she vigilantly peeled every bit of wax from his body and examined the pinkened skin underneath.

"No," he said through gritted teeth. "Not *too* much."

"Well, let's see if I can soothe your pain a little." Returning to her discarded gown, she took the last of her props from the pocket—a small vial of sweet-smelling ointment, also provided by Agnet.

She uncapped and tipped the bottle, pouring a palm full, then she settled on the bed beside Svartan and began to massage his shoulders and chest. She was careful as she moved over the minor burns on his chest and stomach, her stroke soothing and gentle. When she reached his cock, she grasped it and kissed the soft head while sliding her hand down his shaft. She teased her tongue over the tip of his cock and then swallowed him deep, sucking hard until he was thrusting against the back of her throat.

Gwyneth released him and began to massage his cock with the exotically scented oil. His penis was beautiful, glistening with oil and flushed dark from the blood coursing through it. She rubbed up and down with long pulls, and very soon Svartan was cursing some more. His jaw was so tight she feared his bone might pop through the drawn skin.

He gripped her homemade ropes with his fingers and his arm muscles were rigid. His toes curled, too, and the bands of muscle in his legs were like iron.

He can't withstand this. I'm going to win! Gwyneth's heart rose like a bird flying up from earth to sky. Yet in the same instant a dark, heavy feeling wrenched her heart. She wanted her daughter's freedom and her own, but she would actually miss this horrifying monster who held her captive, this demon who played games with peoples' lives. How was that possible?

She slammed her mind shut on such ponderings. This was no time to consider anything but achieving her goal—his orgasm. She'd taken Svartan far enough with her hand; now it was time to straddle this horse and ride him across the finish line.

Gwyneth released his slick cock, and the man grunted in disappointment. She crawled over him, guided his tip to her aching, wet pussy and slipped him inside. Sitting upright, she very slowly settled down on top of him, engulfing him in her hot depths. She braced her hands against his slick chest as she lifted her body almost all the way off his rigid cock, then pushed down onto it again.

Rising and falling on him, she drew him ever closer to the edge. She clenched her muscles tight around him, holding him in the hard grasp of her body, and thought she could feel the very texture of his cock with her inner muscles. She pressed down hard, enveloping him to the very base of his shaft. It felt so good to have him inside her, filling her completely.

Gwyneth leaned forward, changing the angle of her thrusts. Her breasts dipped to brush against his face and he sought a nipple blindly, drawing it into his mouth. He suckled her as he fucked her—or was she fucking him, since she was the one on top and in control?—his mouth drawing on her with hard tugs that sent a sweet ache down to her pussy.

If it was possible, her body clutched him even harder as if she would fuse herself to him and become one. The excited fluttering in her belly, which had been increasing from the moment she entered the room, strengthened and grew. It was as if many individual birds were gathering together into one enormous flock. And then all of a sudden they exploded upward in a mighty surge that carried her with them.

Gwyneth flew. She cried out and threw her head back, arching her neck. Her breast pulled free of his mouth. Her body beat against his with the force of a storm lashing against a rock. Was he impervious to her fierce rain? How could he not join her in ecstasy? She opened her eyes and looked down at him. Oh, but he was close, so close, she could tell.

His eyes were squeezed tight shut and his body was rigid as

if she was punishing him rather than bringing him pleasure. *Just a little longer. A little longer.* She moved her slippery pussy up and down. She was so very wet from coming, her juices covered him.

It's like spinning, she thought. *A steady hand makes smooth, even thread.* She pumped him as she would propel the treadle on a wheel, and she leaned close and added soft words as if singing a spinning tune.

"Come now. Let go. It's what you want, what you need. Don't fight it any longer. Give in to what you need. Come. Come. Come."

He made a strangled sound in his throat and hurled more of those harsh-sounding foreign words at her. And suddenly she wanted him to come with every fiber of her being, not just because of the bet, although the knowledge of it was never out of her mind, but because she wanted to see his face when he was transported with rapture.

"Come, sweetheart, come. Please come for me." She repeated the soothing litany and sped the pace of her thrusts.

And then, just as she was certain she had him, just as she could swear she felt his cock swelling inside her, ready to release, Svartan yelled, "Enough! Your time is up."

Gwyneth was so intent and focused on their bodies moving in unison that she blinked in surprise at the abrupt interruption. Her gaze snapped to the hourglass on the nightstand, which she'd insisted on turning the moment after they'd entered the room.

Sure enough, he was right. The top glass was empty and the bottom one full of white grains of sand. Despair rushed through her. How could she have miscalculated so badly? If she'd only spent a little less time on the wax or the massage, she would have had time to bring him to a conclusion. He'd nearly been there. One or two more twists of her hips even now and he'd...

She couldn't resist doing it even as she thought it.

"I said, enough. Your allotted time is over. If I come now, it does not change our bargain. You still lose." His voice was as harsh as his angular face, without a trace in it of the man she'd thought she was beginning to know.

Gwyneth rose up, disengaging from his cock. The thick, heavy thing flopped against his belly like a club. It was red and purple and shining wet. Come oozed from the tip, leaving a little white puddle on his stomach.

She vaulted off the bed and hurriedly picked up her dress from the floor.

"Untie me," he demanded gruffly.

Ignoring him, she dressed and jammed her feet into her slippers then she headed for the door.

"I said, untie me!" he roared.

"I'm sorry, that's not part of the bargain. My two hours are up." She smiled in bitter satisfaction as the door closed behind her.

Chapter Fifteen

Damn the bloody bargain! What had he been thinking of to make such a senseless deal, one that ensured he lost no matter which way it went? He had gravely miscalculated his ability to charm Gwyneth into falling in love with him—a stupid, stupid plan. Her only thought was of escape, and her only feeling toward him, disgust. Even as she rode him to her climax, she'd been imagining leaving him.

She would never love him, no matter how much he loved her. He would always be an obstacle to her and her daughter's freedom. These thoughts had broken over him in a depressing wave as he'd freed himself from the braided restraints and had torn the blindfold from his eyes.

He could see that now, and it made it impossible for him to face her again. Several days had passed following their second session, and Ragnorak hadn't been able to bring himself to visit Gwyneth or Brea. He had no idea what they were up to in the house or grounds while he went about his usual daily business. It gave him a taste of how it would be to return to his solitary life. Extremely unpleasant.

In the past, Karnak had frequently suggested this widow or that as a possible wife, strongly hinting it was time to find someone with a child to be his queen. Ragnorak had been willing to meet the many women Karnak and his wife had put forth, but had not found one who appealed to him. Any match he made would be a marriage of convenience, and he simply hadn't been ready for that yet. He'd put off the decision by claiming, quite honestly, too much work to accomplish. He'd devoted himself to the building efforts and the government and had tabled the discussion of wives and heirs...until he had quite accidentally met Gwyneth.

The beautiful, golden-haired woman had turned his world upside down and changed his life. Now she was about to leave him alone again and he would never, ever be able to get over her.

One more time together. One final lovemaking—if one could call it that when one half of the couple engaged in the act felt no love at all—then he would lose her and lose darling Brea, who was becoming increasingly precious to him. There was nothing he could do about it. Even if he could hold out and refuse to come, Ragnorak realized now that he could not imprison these two bright spirits in the underworld forever.

He had to let them go.

But maybe he could make one last push to convince Gwyneth to care for him and learn to love this world as much as her own. He had to at least try.

And to have any chance of success, he needed to see her. Thrusting aside the papers he couldn't concentrate on anyhow, he leapt to his feet. It was time to end this stupid game full of half-truths and hidden agendas. He needed to be honest with her, tell her everything that was in his heart and ask her forgiveness as well as her understanding. Perhaps then she'd at least see him as a man with feelings, a flawed man, maybe, but perhaps not totally unworthy of her respect. Love could grow from there...couldn't it?

Filled with a sense of urgency after a week of avoiding the issue, he strode toward the door, wrenching it open so quickly that the fists about to rap on its other side pounded his chest instead. Gwyneth's impatient little fists.

His heart missed a beat. *She's come to me*, he thought in awe. But his triumph only lasted an instant, for the beautiful face turned up to his was ravaged by distress. She wore only her nightgown, which she had clearly either forgotten about or didn't care about in her rush to get to him. Her fingers twisted in his coat, grasping the fabric as if it was her lifeline.

"Please, Svartan! I beg you! I'll do anything if you'll just cure her!"

"Cure who?" Bewildered, shocked by her anguish, he covered her hands with his to calm her, gently detaching them from their vice-like grip on his coat.

"Brea!" she cried, as if he should have known.

Something heavy seemed to fall into the pit of his stomach. This time it was his hands that gripped convulsively. "Brea? What's wrong with her?"

"I don't know!" Gwyneth said in despair. She tugged his hand, urging him along the uneven passage in the direction of her own quarters. As they hurried together, she added intensely, "I've never seen her like this, so ill and distressed. You have to cure her."

"I do?" Startlement as well as fear made his voice harsh, and she clearly took it for stubbornness.

"I know you care for her," she whispered. Tears flowed unchecked down her face. He doubted she even noticed, which made his fear for the baby all the greater. "Please don't take your anger at me out on her..."

"I would never do that."

Something in those words seemed to get through to her. For the first time she glanced at him with more hope than despair. "Then you will help her?"

Ragnorak ran his free hand through his hair. "If I can..."

By then they were at her bedchamber door, and she bolted inside, still tugging him by the hand. Agnet rose from her seat by the cradle and stood quietly to one side while Gwyneth rushed to the cradle.

Fearing what he would see, Ragnorak followed her.

The baby wasn't crying. But her perfect little face had two bright red spots on each cheek. She was twisting with discomfort, as if trying to throw off her covers, tossing her head from side to side. Her breathing sounded erratic and stentorian.

Gwyneth reached down to the child's forehead. "Feel her," she commanded. "She's burning with fever."

Brea's skin was undoubtedly hot and dry, dangerously so. Her little face puckered. She tried to cry, then had to pause to breathe instead. Ragnorak felt his chest tighten.

"You will save her?" Gwyneth demanded.

Ragnorak looked up at her, frowning. "What makes you think I can?"

The eyes he'd seen clouded and hot with passion hid nothing now. She had neither the will nor the ability to try. He saw a twinge of fear and anger, a disbelief that he would really refuse her request.

She said matter-of-factly, "You're the most powerful being I've ever met or heard of. You can turn straw into gold, travel instantly between realms through layers of impenetrable rock. Surely you can make one sick baby well?"

"Gwyneth," he began helplessly. It seemed impossible to explain that the powers he'd always taken for granted did not make him an omnipotent being, some kind of god. He began to see himself through her eyes and, for probably the first time in his life, was afraid of not living up to someone's expectations. He drew a deep breath. "Those kinds of powers are inherent in my royal blood. It is a strength, not a magic. We have an affinity with the elements. I can manipulate them to make straw gold, to compress the air to travel, and change the rocks and earth to let us through. That, I don't even need to think about. But I've never healed a sick child in my life. Here, we do not get ill."

She frowned in disbelief, glancing at Agnet for confirmation. "What, never?"

He shook his head, his gaze drifting back to Brea.

"Then you have no doctors? If you cannot help her, there is no one else?"

Again, he shook his head, seeing out of the corner of his eyes that she clawed at her face with despair. "She might die, Svartan."

The words came out in a whisper, cutting into his heart.

I killed her, he thought numbly. Knowing nothing, I brought her here. This place is not natural for her. She needs fresh air and sunshine to live. I brought her to darkness and death. And if she dies, Gwyneth could do so as well...

"We won't let her die," he said between his teeth. Reaching into the cot, he pulled the covers off the baby and threw them on the floor. Then he began to unbutton her clothing.

"What are you doing?" Gwyneth demanded, catching at his hand in fear.

"She's too hot! The heat is killing her. So we must make her cooler. Agnet, fetch some fresh cold water."

"But..." Clearly torn between tradition and a need to do something, she stared at him while Agnet hurried away. "You really think it will help?"

"At this stage, I don't see that it can harm her."

Gwyneth nodded once and picked the baby up. By the time Agnet returned with a little tub full of water, Brea was undressed. Unquestioning now, Gwyneth knelt by the tub and held her child in the cool, clean water.

Brea cried at the shock, but Gwyneth kept cupping water over her body, sprinkling it gently over her face and head.

I did this, Ragnorak kept thinking. *I made her ill.* Forcing himself to speak, he said, "When she's cooler, we'll take her back."

"Back?" Gwyneth repeated without comprehension.

"To the surface. To her own world. I never thought of Elohim making her ill."

There was a pause. Gwyneth glanced at him over her shoulder, a peculiarly clear look, although her expression was unreadable. "Children get ill," she said. "We try to make them better. Sometimes it works."

Was that an attempt at absolution? It warmed his heart, but he knew it didn't absolve him. As she turned back to the child, Agnet touched his shoulder.

"In the old days," his housekeeper said, "we did get ill. Or so the stories say."

"They're just stories."

"Maybe. But the stories say it was the kings who overcame the illnesses."

"Self-serving propaganda," Ragnorak said impatiently. "Put about by my ancestors."

"Maybe," Agnet said again.

Gwyneth's gaze was fixed on her. "Are you saying that Svartan *can* cure Brea?"

Agnet shrugged. "I'm saying it's a possibility, and maybe one worth trying."

Gwyneth said nothing, merely returned her gaze to the baby. Ragnorak moved closer. It might have been his imagination, but the baby seemed to be breathing more easily.

Her eyes were closed.

"I think she's cooler," Gwyneth said. "More peaceful."

"We must keep her cool," Ragnorak said. "The illness won't disappear with the bathwater. Dress her lightly and we'll take her back."

Unexpectedly, Gwyneth's eyes filled with tears. "Thank you," she whispered. Blindly, she took the proffered towel from Agnet and lifted Brea out of the water, wrapping her loosely in the soft fabric.

She paused. "I'll still need a doctor... As you say, the illness won't vanish with the bathwater. Perhaps it won't vanish with Elohim, either." Taking a deep breath, she held the baby out to Ragnorak. "Please. Heal her."

Ragnorak opened his mouth and closed it again. He looked from her intense, suddenly trusting eyes to Agnet's decisive ones.

"There's nothing to lose," the servant said.

Slowly, Ragnorak took Brea in his arms. Her eyes fluttered open as if she was aware of the change-over. For an instant her eyes looked trustingly into his, a mirror of her mother's.

Ragnorak's throat closed. *I would give the world, my own life, to keep you safe...* With his emotion, a desire to heal rose up so strongly that it was a need, a necessity. Placing his hand on her little chest, he felt the fluttering beat of her heart, the uneven rising and falling of her lungs. He breathed with her, lost his heartbeat in hers. It was as if he felt her internal organs, his mind wishing with all the considerable strength and emotion of which he was capable to sweep the alien illness from her body, the fever from her blood. He sensed all her heat, her angry, bewildered discomfort, and tried to draw it into himself, to free her.

She stopped breathing.

With a jolt, Ragnorak came back to himself, withdrawing in terror whatever unknown and uncontrolled power he'd exposed her to. With a cry of utter despair and loss, he almost threw her into Gwyneth's arms, desperate to get the child away from him. Gwyneth's cry seemed to echo his, and so deep was his grief that it was several moments before he realized her voice conveyed only joy and relief.

As he stared, stunned, at mother and child, Gwyneth's tear-stained face came back into focus. She was smiling.

"I can feel it," she whispered. "She is healed. I knew you could. I knew you would..."

"Imagination," Ragnorak said hoarsely. "I did nothing but wish."

Agnet touched the baby and smiled. "She's breathing normally again. And I can see little sign of fever. Even her color is coming back to normal—pretty, golden little thing that she is."

Quietly, Agnet left the room, leaving Ragnorak and Gwyneth staring in wonder at Brea. Whether it had come from him or not, the child seemed immeasurably better. She was actually asleep in Gwyneth's arms. Trembling with reaction, Gwyneth laid her in the cradle and with the automatic movements of familiarity, began to put a clean diaper on her. That done, ignoring the clothes, she simply replaced the coverlet.

Ragnorak's throat worked. He thought he was going to weep. But instead, words spilled out of his mouth in an agonized whisper. "I'm sorry. I'm so sorry."

Gwyneth straightened, staring at him in genuine incomprehension. "For what? You healed her. I'm convinced you saved her life. I will never forget that, Svartan, never."

"Ragnorak." It came out as a strangled whisper.

"What?"

He couldn't bear the softness in her eyes, which not only forgave him but glistened with gratitude. He swung away from her, saying harshly, "Ragnorak. My true name is Ragnorak. And surely we both know it was I who endangered her in the first place."

He didn't know why he reminded her. She would realize it soon enough when the first rush of relief had passed and she could think straight again. But he needed to be honest now, even though he could hardly bear the emotions tearing him apart. He had to get out of here. Five minutes' solitude and then he would take them back...

Grief swamped him, fighting with the guilt and the relief and a tenderness so profound it rocked him to his core. When she touched him, he gasped, trying to pull farther away from her, but she followed, peering up into his face with wonder.

Her blue eyes were huge and beautiful. He didn't know how he could bear to let her go. But he knew he couldn't keep her. He should never have brought her or the child.

Her hand lifted. Her fingertips brushed his cheek, and he realized it was wet with the tears he hadn't known he'd shed.

"Svartan," she whispered. "Ragnorak..." His name on her lips pierced his soul, filled him with delight and desolation. "My demon... You wept once before, the night we made our bargain. How could I have forgotten that?"

"Because I did. I knew I shouldn't be doing it, and yet I did. I never wavered. Forget it, Gwyneth. I'll make it right."

She smiled, taking what was left of his breath away. "You've already made it right. You gave me Brea's life."

Almost angrily, he burst out, "Can you really not see? I was the one who nearly took it from you! From her! You *must* see—"

"I do see. I see everything now," she whispered, and

stretching up on tip-toe, she kissed his lips, a quick, soft kiss that devastated him.

He closed his eyes. “Gwyneth, you’re killing me. Do you not know how much I love you?”

Her breath touched his lips. “How much?”

“More than my life. More even than my kingdom. So much that it’s unkind to touch me now.”

Tiny kisses peppered his lips, silencing him. When her arms came around his neck, drawing his head down to her, he gasped again in an effort to break free. It was no good. The arms that reached up to push her away seized her close to him instead, clutched her as if he’d never let her go.

She gave a tiny sigh, her tongue slipping between his parted lips, and Ragnorak was lost. He devoured her mouth, and with her every eager response, he took more, sinking into the blissful agony of all the desire and love and loss that Gwyneth now embodied.

“You would do this?” He pulled away and stared into her eyes. “You would give me this third, last night? Before I take you home?”

“I give you it, and gladly.” Her voice trembled. “I want it, my Ragnorak, my demon. I’ve always wanted you…”

He made a last effort to think, to be strong, because he knew emotion and sheer reaction were drowning them both. He knew that the sweet, urgent woman in his arms would probably not love him when she awoke. But her pebbled breasts were rubbing against his chest, her mouth kissed with passion, her tongue teasing and delighting his. She pushed and swayed against his raging erection, arousing him almost to the point of no return.

Groaning, he tore his mouth free. “Brea,” he got out. “We cannot leave Brea.”

"We won't. Make love to me here. She's asleep, and I'll know as soon as she wakes."

Her parted lips were red and lush from kissing him. Her eyes shone. Her golden hair tumbled in tangles around her face and shoulders. She had never been more beautiful to him.

"You are so lovely," he whispered. "My golden girl." He touched her hair, following its tangled progress to her half-naked shoulder. "You're like the gold we spun all those months ago. Like sunshine. You burn me and draw me at once."

Her smooth skin was warm, shivering beneath his fingers as he slid his hands under the shoulder of her nightgown and let it fall around her elbows to reveal her wonderful breasts.

He kissed her throat, her clavicle. She threw her head back with such abandon that he couldn't doubt her arousal or her pleasure. Tenderly, he cupped one heavy breast, loving the feel of her hard, distended nipple under the pad of his thumb. Her tiny moan was like music, driving him to bend his head farther and take the other nipple into his mouth.

Her clutching hands released his hair, dropped from his neck so that her nightgown fell the rest of the way to the floor. He straightened to look at her, completely naked for him. His moisture glistened on the tip of one breast. Her own moisture trickled down her parted inner thigh. He had never seen anything so arousing as this lovely, naked woman, so desperate for his embrace that her pussy wept.

He touched her mound, easing his hand between her thighs, and her breath caught and held. He bathed his hand in her moisture, losing himself in the heady heat of her folds and valleys, discovering the hard, swollen nub of her pleasure and gliding over it until she moaned.

Her hands plucked at his coat, tugging it from his shoulders. Shrugging it off, he could wait no longer, but lifted her in his arms and strode with her to the bed he'd fashioned for her a lifetime ago.

Even as he laid her among the pillows, she was unlacing his shirt, sliding her hot, eager palms under it to find his naked chest. With such encouragement it took only an instant to lose the rest of his clothes, even with the distraction of her busy mouth on his nipples, teasing and biting. As he settled over her, nestling his body and his aching cock between her legs, she writhed under him, her eyes warm and clouded and pleading. Taking her face between his hands, he kissed her long and deeply, savoring her instant, eager response. He made love to her mouth, letting his caressing hands move down her body.

Her fingers ran up and down his back, making his whole body undulate and somehow, before he quite meant it to happen, the head of his cock had entered her pussy. It contracted around him, hot and pulsing. With a moan, she pushed her hips upward, taking him further into her welcoming wetness. He couldn't help thrusting all the way inside her, right up to his balls. Her gasp of pleasure rang in his ears. She smiled up at him, wicked and joyful, and he paused, savoring for the first time in his life, a moment of pure, unspoiled happiness.

It couldn't last, of course. The tragedy of parting was too close, but he held on to the memory, because he knew for that instant, she loved him.

She reached up with her mouth and kissed him. He began to move inside her with long, tender strokes. He had never had this before, the freedom to love her without fighting impending orgasm, to explore her with no agenda but to bring her joy. His cock quickly found the place she liked best and from then on he made certain to find it with every thrust and every sweet, circling grind. His reward came not only in her moans and cries of pleasure, but in the increasingly powerful grip of her internal muscles around his cock as she squeezed and caressed him.

Lost in the blissful world that contained only the two of them, he slid constantly up and down her tight, wet pussy, building the rapture. There was no fight for control, only the two of them undulating and writhing together to the same, frantic end. Her nails dug into his buttocks as she pulled him into her, desperate to increase the pace, to find the ultimate pleasure. Ragnorak moved faster, hanging desperately on to the shreds of care and tenderness as he drove into her ever harder and faster.

"Ragnorak," she whispered. "Oh, Ragnorak, I'm..."

So was he. As she convulsed around him, thrilling him as much by the sound of his name bursting from her ecstatic lips, he let everything go at last. In three wild, desperate strokes he joined her orgasm, releasing his seed into her in an explosion of joy so violent that it shook his whole body. There wasn't a nerve ending, not so much as a finger tip, that didn't feel soaked in pleasure. And through it all, her body jerked under him, around him, and her voice cried out in bliss.

There may even have been an instant of unconsciousness. But as he came back to some kind of sense, at least he retained enough care to move his weight off Gwyneth's body. However, she clung to him, twisting with him so that they lay on their sides face to face with his cock still buried deep inside her.

She smiled at him with such tender mischief that his rapidly beating heart turned over in his breast. "You lost," she crowed. "At last, you lost!"

And he smiled back and kissed her mouth. "No I didn't."

Chapter Sixteen

"The king had to send her away, of course. Just after the child was born. He had to marry, you see, and the disgusting underdweller just wasn't suitable."

"Indeed." Midas nodded to his steward, who pushed the ancient, wizened old woman into a chair, none too gently. The king had thought at first they were really dredging the bottom of the barrel with this old hag. It wasn't even worth torturing her, and in any case he was fed up listening to lies extracted on the rack from people who'd have said anything just to stop the pain.

But there was something about the old woman. Midas began to wonder if he didn't recognize her. At any rate, she really did sound like an old palace servant, and when she claimed to remember the demon child and his mother, he felt oddly inclined to believe her.

"Why wasn't she suitable?" he asked.

The old woman regarded him with scorn. "A whore from the magical realm? She could claim all the royal blood she liked, but we all knew what she was."

"Hmmm. And did she mind being sent away?"

"She didn't mind going," the old woman said with a cackle of laughter. "But you should have heard her trying to persuade the king to go with her. Told him he'd find incredible riches in her realm. Beyond his imagination, she said. Apparently, in her world they trampled underfoot the gold and gems that we so prize. The maids made necklaces out of stones bigger than the crown jewels. Apparently!"

Midas sat up. He even stopped drumming his fingers. "Indeed?"

The old woman shrugged. "If you were naive enough to believe her."

"You didn't?"

"Would you?" scoffed the hag.

"Did the king?" Midas countered.

"Don't know. The whore and her child were both gone by morning."

"Interesting..." His mind moved beyond the immediate problem of getting Gwyneth back to the prospect of a brand new kingdom full of new wealth for the taking. If he could wrest it from his half-brother. If he could *find* his bloody brother.

"I don't suppose," Midas sighed, "that you know the name of this woman's child?"

The old lady's eyebrows rose. "Svartan," she said. "She called him Svartan in my presence. Ungodly, un-human name."

Midas began to smile. "Never discount the old and ugly," he said to no one in particular. He stood and raised his voice commandingly. "Oh, Svartan! I summon you! Come to me now!"

Gwyneth, her head propped up on her hand so that she could gaze down upon her strange, wonderful lover, played her fingers around his broad, strong chest.

"You think you've won?" she teased. "I know we didn't use the timer, but that was never two hours."

"Before, I could only lose," he said. "You would leave me or you would shun me. Tonight I could only win."

"Because you changed the rules of the game?"

"Because tonight I wasn't playing."

Her heart turned over, constricting her throat. "Neither was I," she whispered. It had just seemed so right. Brea's sudden, terrifying illness and even more sudden recovery had brought things into proper perspective. She hadn't taken him into her bed from gratitude, however much of that she owed him. He was a man, a strange, compelling, tortured man, who'd made a mistake and was sorry. A man she could swear loved her, even before he spoke the words. He'd even given her his real name and all the power over him that he imagined it gave her. He'd said he would take them back. And she knew then, as she should always have known, that she loved him, too.

It had always been there, that feeling, incipient but powerful, even in those early nights, spinning straw into gold, when he'd kissed her and aroused her and pleasured her. Wanting him, she'd married the king, but had never stopped wanting him, even through the worst of her anger.

And now she had him. He'd made love to her like an angel, giving her an ecstasy she'd never known and never imagined. And she'd made him come at last. She could still feel his seed inside her, trickling around his semi-hard cock which still nestled in her pussy.

Lowering her head, she kissed his mouth, almost with wonder. Then, feeling his cock twitch and grow once more inside her, she pushed him onto his back and climbed astride him.

"So if we're not playing, what now?" she said breathlessly.

In an instant, he'd rolled her over and taken his own weight on his elbows. "Now we have more than that paltry two hours," he said, and slid out of her, tracing a line of kisses down her breasts and stomach. Pausing only to part her thighs, he continued on his way, teasing her by kissing everywhere but her pussy.

He said, "The very first time I made you come was like this." And he latched his mouth to her lower lips in a strong, sensual kiss that made her cry out. "But it seems I'm losing my touch."

"No," she gasped. "I've just learned more. From you."

"So now I have to work for your climaxes?"

"Yes, please..."

Laughing softly, he licked her clitoris, and she clutched his head in abandon. She let her hips move as they wanted to, drinking in the rhythm of his kisses as he pleasured her. When he slid one finger inside her, the tension grew. When another joined it and he began to suck her clitoris, lashing it with his tongue as he slid those fingers up and down her slick pussy, she began to come. And kept coming in one long, searing stream that she thought would never end.

Only when it finally calmed did he rear up on his knees, smiling wolfishly as he wiped her juices off his face with the back of his hand and pushed his hot, rigid cock inside her. She welcomed him with an exhausted purr.

"Again," he said, and rode her hard. She didn't think she could. She concentrated on his pleasure, thrusting upward to meet his every stroke, squeezing and teasing his cock with her still trembling internal muscles. And she could feel his galloping pleasure, the tightening of his heavy balls as she avidly stroked them. And her own climax rose up swiftly with his. Some instinct propelled her upward into a sitting position so that she could grab around his neck and kiss him, open mouthed and gasping as they came, grinding and convulsing together.

Eventually, dragging her mouth free, she buried it in his

shoulder instead, smiling.

"I love you, Ragnorak."

He grew very still, as if she'd shocked him. Did he really not know? But when she would have raised her head to gaze at him, he held her face into his shoulder. His body jerked and she wondered if he was weeping again.

He said something muffled. It might have been, "I've never known such happiness." She hoped it was. Fiercely, she wanted to give him every happiness of which he was capable.

At last he raised her head to kiss her, a long, sweet kiss. "Gwyneth..."

Brea gave a snuffle and as one, both their heads turned toward the cot. Gwyneth didn't need to ask him to move. He withdrew at once and, even through her anxiety, she welcomed the spasm of pleasure induced by his cock sliding out of her. Naked, she leapt off the bed and covered the few paces to the cot.

Brea grinned at her and kicked off the cover.

Gwyneth laughed and picked her up. At once, she began snouting in Gwyneth's shoulder, looking for milk.

"Is she all right?" Ragnorak asked.

"Fine. She's just hungry. The fever's completely gone." Gwyneth flung a little gown over the baby's head and brought her back to the bed. There she paused. "Do you mind if I feed her here?"

Ragnorak shook his head slowly. A small, curiously sad smile played around his mouth. "No. I'd like you to."

She climbed back into bed and settled Brea on to her breast while Ragnorak watched. After a moment, his arm came 'round her shoulder, gentle and cherishing, encompassing both of them, and Gwyneth's happiness was complete.

"Idiot," snarled Midas, shooing the old woman from his presence. "That can't be his name."

Or had he really gone mad to be imagining he could summon this semi-mythical brother from some magical underworld by the speaking of his name? Whether the name was wrong, or his memory of what to do with it, "Svartan" had certainly not worked. Any more than "Rumpelstiltskin" had worked for stupid Gwyneth.

But as the door closed behind the shuffling old hag, he was again sure he was right. The memory, stirred by the old woman's genuine ramblings, reformed. He saw again his sick, old father clutching him, gibbering nonsensical words that had meant nothing then and everything now. "Just say his name. Say his name and he's got to come. His name is..."

Not Svartan, no! But he almost had it! Almost...

"Say his name and he's got to come. His name is...*Ragnorak*!"

"Yes! Got you!" Midas whispered.

Leaping to his feet, he walked to the middle of the room. "Ragnorak, my brother, I summon you! Come to me now!"

Chapter Seventeen

As he disappeared from beside her, the echo of Gwyneth's cry rang in Ragnorak's ears. The power inside that allowed him to shift rock and compress air was beyond his control now. He whirled through space against his will, tumbling through the air and landing on a hard stone floor. He dragged himself up from an awkward sprawl to stand on shaky legs and face his summoner.

Midas, garbed in gold and wearing a lavish necklace of jewels in a gold setting, stood before him looking every inch a monarch. But looking into his eyes, Ragnorak could see his character was weak, spoiled, selfish, cruel and all thing unkingly. He didn't deserve to rule and certainly didn't deserve a wife and daughter like Gwyneth and Brea.

Ragnorak had been unable to resist the call of his name, but that didn't mean he had to bow down and obey this man like some spirit uncorked from a bottle. He was a king in his own right, ruler of the entire underworld. He straightened his shoulders, aware of his naked torso and glad he'd happened to put on a pair of drawers before being abruptly pulled from his bed.

"You called my name...brother?" He glared with hard-eyed intensity at Midas.

The other man glanced nervously at the guards standing

nearby and ordered, “Seize him.”

Obediently, two soldiers approached Ragnorak. He held up a negligent hand, to solidify the air and block their approach. He was behind an invisible shield of his own making as he’d been the time he’d come to claim Gwyneth.

“You may have the power to summon me, Midas, but you can’t imprison me. Our mutual father asked my mother to grant this boon—a bond between us, if you will—hoping I might come to your aid should you ever truly need me. Mother graciously granted the request, weaving the power of summoning into my name. But this is a one-time use only. You can’t use the summons again.” The last bit was a lie, but Midas didn’t need to know that. “Now what is it you want from me?”

“My wife back! She’s been imprisoned in your realm by some demon. Find her. Return her and my daughter to me at once.”

Did the man really not know it was he who had taken Gwyneth? Ragnorak studied his face and weighed his options. He meant to return Brea and Gwyneth to the topside world anyway, but not to this undeserving man. Somehow he must secure their freedom from Midas, making certain Gwyneth and Brea lived happily at last.

“I could grant that request, but I’m not here to serve you. This is a negotiation between us.”

“I don’t play games unless I know I’ll win,” Midas said flatly. “And a king doesn’t need to negotiate. He takes.”

“He negotiates with the monarch of another kingdom unless he wishes to provoke a war.” Ragnorak imbued his words and glare with as much threat as he could muster, which was considerable. He didn’t really intend to create a conflict between the lower and upper worlds, having worked too hard to overcome the enmity between them. But again, what Midas didn’t know could be used to manipulate him.

"As I said, I could return your wife and child," he continued, "but I sense there are things you'd find more valuable. My realm is full of the minerals and stones you apparently deem valuable." He indicated the opulent neckpiece Midas wore. "Gold is a poor mineral as far as my people are concerned. It's not hard enough to be of great value to us."

"You're suggesting I trade my adored wife and baby for jewels and gold? What sort of man would do such a thing?"

"A man who loved a woman only when he thought she could spin straw into gold. I'm telling you now, Gwyneth does not have that ability. I fulfilled the task you set for her. The woman has no special powers beyond what every woman has."

"You lie. You're the one who took her and you want to keep her for yourself!"

"No. I want her to be free, and I'm willing to bargain for her freedom." An idea flamed to life in his mind, a way to appease Midas while securing Gwyneth's safety.

"What kind of a bargain? I have a kingdom that skates on the verge of financial collapse. I would need great incentive to sacrifice my cherished family for wealth to support my country."

Ragnorak folded his arms over his bare chest and stared at his half-brother. "Your people will admire you for making such a noble sacrifice on their behalf," he said dryly. "How much would make it worth your while to divorce Gwyneth—who, incidentally, has already divorced you according to our laws—sever your parental rights over Brea and allow them to leave the palace and live comfortably in a home of their own?"

Realizing he had something Ragnorak desired seemed to restore some of Midas's lost bravado. He strode toward him, heels clicking on the flagstones, and stopped only when he reached the invisible barrier. From several feet away, he stared at Ragnorak. "You fancy yourself in love with the wench? How amusing. What is it about you lowborn demons that draws you to the light of our world? You don't belong here, and no one from here can ever belong to you."

Ragnorak was growing impatient. He wanted to make the deal and be done with it, cut Gwyneth cleanly from his life and slink away to lick his wounds. "I know that," he said through gritted teeth. "Thus the offer of a deal."

He could almost see the wheels turning in Midas's head as he tried to calculate how much he could get away with. Ragnorak realized right then that no matter what figure he came up with, however many bushels of diamonds, emeralds, sapphires, rubies or pounds of gold and silver, Midas would always think he should have held out for more. And Ragnorak could never feel certain Gwyneth and Brea were truly safe.

"This arrangement will be ongoing," Ragnorak suggested. "I'll return Gwyneth and Brea to the castle and fill one storeroom with gold. In a month, my proxy will check on their wellbeing. If their situation meets with his approval, I'll fill your storeroom again. After that I'll check on their progress yearly. As long as they're safe, secure and content, I'll supply a roomful of metals or gemstones, per your request."

"What happens if either should fall ill through no fault of mine?"

Ragnorak smiled, and he knew his smile could chill the blood and make a man cower in fear. "You should hope they remain in good health—and happy. Do we have a deal?"

Midas paused a moment, searching for an angle, a way to push for just a little bit more than the already generous offer.

"My patience wears thin," Ragnorak thundered, leaning toward the other man. "And if I leave now, I keep everything. The only way you would wrest Gwyneth or the gold from me would be through full scale war between my nation and yours. Trust me. You don't want to rouse my ire." He sent out a wave of power from his hand that shattered the stone mantelpiece with a crack, sending shards of rock and dust raining to the floor.

"Yes. All right. It's a deal," Midas agreed quickly. "A yearly supply of gold, and I'll leave the woman alone."

"Done!" Ragnorak released the protecting air around him and stepped forward to grasp his half-brother's hand and give it a firm shake. Then he sent out a powerful wave that shaped both air and stone to his will and disappeared with a clap of thunder.

Gwyneth had been pacing the room with Brea held to her shoulder, rubbing the baby's back for what felt like hours, ever since Ragnorak had inexplicably disappeared from beside them.

She'd felt the suction of a vortex as his solid form evaporated to be replaced by nothing but air, but she and Brea had not been pulled along with him to wherever he'd gone. Why would he leave them so abruptly between one breath and the next? She found it impossible to believe he'd gone of his own will. Some force had drawn him away from her—but to where and would he return?

At last she could take worrying in solitude no longer and was about to go find Karnak and explain the situation. Perhaps he or Agnet would have some insight into where their lord had disappeared to. Gwyneth laid the now sleeping baby back in her cradle and turned to walk from the room. At that moment, Ragnorak reappeared with a whoosh that set the air rippling as if a stiff breeze had swept through the room.

He stood in the center of the bedroom—no longer a fearsome figure garbed in deadly black, but a half-nude and vulnerable man. His guise had been stripped away, and Gwyneth knew him now for who he really was with all his strengths and weaknesses. Ragnorak was a ruler who cared for his people and tirelessly worked toward a better world for them.

His kingly mantle made him a bit arrogant at times, but beneath it was a streak of self-doubt about his ability to lead. He was acutely aware of his half-blood status and felt somewhat of an outsider even among his own people. He was passionate, lonely, brave, reserved, powerful, uncertain. He was so many things, but most importantly, he was hers.

She rushed to him and threw her arms around him, pressing her cheek to his hard chest and listening to his strong heartbeat. "What happened?"

"I was called away." A humorless chuckle vibrated through his chest. He held her for a brief moment before grasping her shoulders and pushing her back.

Gwyneth looked into his face. "By whom?"

"A relative." He met her gaze, then glanced at Brea sleeping in the cradle. "There's something I haven't told you. I guess now I can't put it off any longer."

Her hands rested at his waist and she rubbed her palms over his warm skin. "Tell me."

"As I said, I needed an heir because I can't reproduce, being of mixed blood. My human father was King Gordia." He fell silent, waiting for her to understand the import of that.

It took a moment for Gwyneth's numb mind to make the connection. "King Gordia, Midas's father? You are Midas's half-brother." Her mind whirled at the concept.

He nodded. "My name is imbued with summoning power, which is why I never share it. But somehow Midas discovered it and called me to him just now."

Gwyneth's stomach clenched as she tried to sort through what this meant. "Does it give him control over you? Do you have to do his bidding?"

Ragnorak paused before answering. "Something like that. We've made an arrangement at any rate. I will return you and

Brea to him, but he will divorce you so you might live your life the way you choose—at last, no husband or father controlling you."

He smiled slightly as he waited for her gratitude.

"You will 'return us' just like that, like property or possessions you've tired of and want to give away?" Hurt was followed quickly by anger bubbling up inside her. Here he was, offering her the gift of freedom but treating her once more like an object to be manipulated and moved as every man in her life had done.

"You're not pleased?" His smile weakened at the corners.

"You didn't ask me. You told me this and expected me to be ecstatic." She took her hands from his waist and folded her arms over her chest.

"It's what you wanted. For Brea's health and yours, you can't live underground, and you said you didn't want to return to Midas." His smile was long gone and a frown furrowed his brow.

"I don't. But I also don't want you to decide for me."

The frown became a scowl and he looked nearly as formidable as when he was dressed in black. "There's no decision to be made. This is best for you and the child, and an agreement has been made. You will go to the topside world where you belong."

She wanted to continue to argue, to refuse to go and remind him they'd exchanged words of love not so very long ago. But she also knew he was right about the long term effects of living underground. This world was not hers or Brea's. Torn by the impossible situation, she sought some solution, but Ragnorak didn't give her a chance to think of one.

"The deal's been struck. You're leaving now. Take the child in your arms so I might send you back." His voice was as hard as granite. He picked up his discarded shirt from the floor and put it on, then shoved his legs into trousers and boots.

Gwyneth spoke not a word as she lifted Brea from the cradle and held her close. Her world was spinning and he hadn't even sent her through the vortex yet. Her desire for her daughter's freedom warred with her own wish to remain bound by love. On her own, she would live the rest of her life in this underworld, sacrificing sun, sky and fresh air to remain with her lover, but she had Brea to consider. And right now Ragnorak was so cold he felt like a stranger again—one who was pushing her away with his rigid, distant demeanor.

He stood before her now, fully clothed in black once more, and spoke in a coolly polite voice. "I'm sorry for all the trouble I've caused you. I want you to know I've enjoyed your company. I'll miss you and Brea, but this is for the best, as I'm certain you'll agree."

Before she could respond, reach out to him or even formulate a thought, he was gone—or actually she was, rushing through space. He hadn't even taken her hand. She didn't know he could do his magic without leading her through the space he made between the worlds.

Gwyneth felt a shock up her legs as her feet landed on solid ground. She clutched Brea tighter and fought for balance. The baby let out a squawk of annoyance.

Gwyneth looked around and found she was in the garden of the castle. It was nighttime. The moon shone overhead, a beautiful array of stars sparkled and a light breeze caressed her face and ruffled her hair. She lifted her face and inhaled a deep draught of the first fresh air she'd tasted in weeks. It smelled like freedom...and felt like a prison sentence. She was back where she'd wanted to be, but without her beloved demon.

She would never see Ragnorak again.

From the way he'd acted, he didn't even care.

Chapter Eighteen

Ragnorak lifted the bottle and drank. He'd long since given up on pouring the wine into a goblet. What was the point?

Or the point in getting dressed when he wasn't planning on leaving his room?

Or the point in living, really, since all light had been extinguished from his life?

He knew he was acting like a weak, miserable, useless, lovelorn, pitiable bastard, but straightening his spine and being a man was too exhausting to consider. At least no one could fault him for abandoning his duties to Elohim. He accomplished all his tasks in a timely manner, met with various committees and signed official documents. If he chose to collapse and drink himself into a stupor on his own time, it was his business.

He let out a loud belch and took another drink.

There was a sharp rap on his chamber door and Karnak entered before Ragnorak could snarl, "Go away."

His steward, secretary, friend stood staring at him until Ragnorak was forced to look up at him through bleary eyes. "What is it?"

"You're a mess, and it's time you pulled yourself together." Apparently Karnak was now also acting as his conscience or perhaps his mother.

"Is it?" he drawled and slumped back into the chair, taking

another pull at the bottle.

"Yes," Karnak stated flatly as he kicked aside an empty bottle and pushed dirty laundry from the other chair to the floor so he could sit. "If you won't let the servants in to clean, you could at least pick up a little."

"I like it like this."

"People are starting to worry. Your nation looks to you. Your confidence is their confidence, and if they doubt your ability to lead..."

Ragnorak glared. "Why should anyone doubt? I haven't shirked my duties or missed any engagements. What do they have to gossip about?"

Karnak pursed his lips and placed his steepled fingers against them for a moment before answering. "I understand what you're going through. Before I married Guzel, when I was much younger, I fell in love once, hard, for a woman quite beyond my reach. The affair was like none other I've ever had," he lowered his voice, "even my beloved Guzel. I would've given my life for that woman, done anything to become what she needed me to be. But it was impossible."

He paused and waited for some reaction. Ragnorak took another drink.

"The point is, at the time I believed I could never recover, never love again. But I found another, a different woman, but a dear one nevertheless. My love for Guzel grew slowly but steadily and now it is greater than the flame I once felt for my youthful love." He paused once more then added, "Svartan, you will find another woman. Look among your own kind this time. There are many who would make you a fine wife and a worthy queen."

Ragnorak threw the bottle across the room, where it crashed against the wall and shattered the mirror, sending shards of glass raining to the floor. "I don't want anyone else. I want *her*!" he roared.

Karnak looked at the destroyed mirror and back to his friend. "In that case, maybe you should find a way to win her."

"I can't! Neither she nor the child could survive down here. I had to let them go."

Karnak exhaled and drummed his fingers on the arm of the chair. "It sounds as if you'd thought this through thoroughly and there's absolutely no solution. Hmm. Surprising that a man with your ingenuity couldn't possibly work out the problem. A little compromise, a little give and take would be out of the question, I suppose." He shrugged and rose to his feet. "Very well. I'm sure you know best."

Ragnorak growled his displeasure at his second-in-command's sarcastic comments. He was in serious pain and deserved sympathy, not flippant remarks. "I've given her up because I love her. I'm giving her a chance at a normal, happy life. Isn't that the heroic thing to do?"

"Certainly, if you want to be a hero who's alone. All I'm saying is, either put the woman from your mind and move on, or go after her and find a way to make it work. But this wallowing is truly pathetic...sire," Karnak drawled, taking liberties only a longtime friend was allowed.

The door closed behind him, and the goblet Ragnorak was no longer using crashed against the door. Ragnorak spat a curse before sinking back into his chair. Karnak didn't know about the other part of the bargain. The gold provided to Midas would ensure the man never tried to invade the underworld. If Ragnorak broke the bargain by taking Gwyneth again, the greedy man might use it as an excuse to forfeit peace between the nations and try for even greater riches.

He pressed his palm against his brow, trying to relieve his headache, but the pressure wouldn't ebb. He hated when

Karnak pointed out the obvious. Of course, he couldn't pine like this forever. He had to get up and move no matter how exhausted he felt. There was always more work to be done and the people needed him to be a leader in all ways. If he couldn't have Gwyneth and Brea, he would devote himself to work instead, tirelessly striving to make Elohim the best place it could be. No weakness. No brooding. No more yearning for the impossible. He could live without love. He'd managed to for years.

Rising from the chair, he went to pick up the shattered glass from the floor.

Gwyenth knelt on the front porch of her little house, scrubbing bird droppings from the floorboards. She glanced up at the red-breasted wrens nesting in the corner of the porch beneath the eaves. Were they the same ones from her father's house? Had they followed her here?

She scowled and clucked her tongue at them. "Go live somewhere else, stupid birds, or at least stop crapping on my floor."

In her cradle nearby, Brea squeaked, her little noises sounding rather like the birds' chirps. Gwyneth tossed her scrub brush into the bucket of soapy water and rose, wiping her hands on her apron. She crossed to the cradle and smiled down at her daughter. "You like the naughty birds?"

Brea gave a nearly toothless grin and waved her hands wildly in the air. Gwyneth couldn't resist her cuteness and scooped her up into her arms, dancing the baby until she giggled and snorted.

Gwyneth held her to her shoulder and jiggled her, singing softly as she gazed across the yard—*her* yard in front of *her* house, dappled in sunlight and shadows from the forest of trees that surrounded the clearing. This was what she'd wanted, her freedom and Brea's to live life without the interference of a man.

Thanks to Ragnorak's bargain with Midas, the details of which she still wasn't clear on, she had it all and was fairly content when she held Brea in her arms like this and surveyed her domain. But she couldn't say she was happy.

There was something missing—someone—and an aching empty place in her heart where he used to be. It was better during the day when she was busy tending house and taking care of the animals and, of course, Brea. But at night, alone in her bed, she missed Ragnorak with a painful twisting of her insides that felt like it might actually kill her. She could scarcely sleep and couldn't put him out of her mind: his hands on her body, his lips on her mouth and his hardness pressed deep inside her.

She'd thought he loved her, but he'd given her up so easily. Maybe she'd never been more than a temporary passion for him. Probably by now he'd found a woman of his own kind and had almost completely forgotten her.

Movement in the thick shadows beneath the pine trees caught her attention. A flash of brilliant scarlet like an oversized cardinal. Gwyneth caught her breath as she recognized Karnak, his silver hair flowing down his back, beckoning her into the forest.

She laid Brea down, ignoring her fussy cries, and descended the steps to walk toward him. "What are you doing here?" It sounded like an accusation rather than a polite greeting, but she couldn't keep the surprise from her voice. She'd never expected to see a denizen of the underworld again.

He smiled and bowed with a flourish. "I'm Svartan's proxy, checking to see how you are."

"I'm fine," she answered absently. "But what are you *doing* here? I thought no one from Elohim could stand the sunlight."

He gestured at the pines. "I can't, thus the shade of the trees, but I didn't want to come at night and disturb you. Everything is well for you then? Midas has fulfilled his promise and found you a home. He has divorced you and severed his custody rights over the child?"

"Yes, he's done all that." Gwyneth nodded. "Although I'm not sure why. What did Ra—Svartan give him in return?"

The man shook his head. "I'm not certain, but I do know this,"—he gazed into her face with his pale eyes—"whatever he's done has been for love of you. You mustn't doubt that. He only wants you both to be safe and well."

"We are, but..." She had no more to add. The subject was too personal.

Karnak hesitated then blurted abruptly, "He suffers. He is slowly wrapping himself in layers of stone, growing as cold and remote as he ever was before he met you. As his friend, I can't stand by and watch this. I wanted you to know."

She should've felt bad for Ragnorak. Instead a bolt of happiness speared through her at the news. He cared. His coolness when he'd bidden her goodbye was just a show. Stepping forward, Gwyneth clasped Karnak's hand. "Thank you. I'm glad you told me."

He dipped his head in acknowledgement. "Now, what are you going to do about it?"

Gwyneth approached the palace gates with some trepidation. She hadn't returned here since her ex-husband had permitted her to leave, but she had a task to perform, an idea to free Ragnorak from whatever hold his half brother had over him. In addition, if she was lucky, she would also convince her stubborn demon lover that there was hope for a future for them together.

She'd left Brea with a neighbor woman while she went forth on this quest and now she walked alone up the paved drive to the castle. Gwyneth noted the gates had recently been plated in gold. She'd already guessed that gold was what Ragnorak had given in order to win her freedom from Midas. The gates confirmed her suspicion that her lover had paid Midas for her new life.

The guards at the gate, wearing expensive cloth of gold, immediately recognized her and bowed deeply as if she were still royalty. Doors opened to permit her entry through the outer wall to the courtyard and then into the castle itself.

One of the footmen rushed to get Wallace to deal with the unexpected arrival of the former queen. As she reached Midas's throne room, the steward was there to intercept her. He bowed politely. "Madam, his highness is busy right now. Perhaps you might visit him at a later date or in a more private setting."

He took her elbow and tried to steer her away from the chamber, but Gwyneth shook off his hand and strode forward. "Out of my way, Wallace. I will see the man now."

Again the guards at the door bowed and opened the door for her as they were trained to do. She marched into the nearly empty throne room to find Midas lounging on his diamond and ruby encrusted throne. Beautiful women sat on cushions on either side of him and one knelt between his legs tending to his cock. No business was being conducted in the throne room today, and Gwyneth guessed this was a party that went on and on.

She knew no tax relief had been given the landowners or their tenants, the artisans or the middle class, despite whatever new riches Midas had accrued from Ragnorak. A bit guiltily, she prayed her suspicions were correct that Midas was tearing through his new wealth as quickly as he had his old. Only if he desired even more would he fall for her bait.

When he saw her, Midas straightened, pushed the woman in front of him aside and tucked his cock into his breeches as he rose from the throne. He waved a dismissive hand and the women hurried from the room.

"Why have you come here?" he demanded, gazing at Gwyneth through bleary, red-shot eyes. "I'm finished with you."

Gwyenth stopped in the center of the room and gazed at him coolly. "As a subject of this country, I've come to seek satisfaction for a wrong that's been done. That is the purpose of the court. Is it not?"

Midas glared. "You have no rights, and you're lucky you've gotten off as lightly as you did after lying to your king about your magic abilities. That's treason. I could've had you beheaded."

Playing with fire, a voice inside her warned, but Gwyneth swallowed the nervous flutter in her throat and pressed forward. She must bait her hook carefully and convince him she had something to gain, too. "As all the world can see, you have palmed off your daughter and me with too little. I need a bigger house and a servant to care for it. It's the least you can do for us. However, I don't wish you to..." She cast a glance around her opulent surroundings. "...go short. And so, I have a proposition to make, a bet I dare you to take."

"A bet?" He laughed. "Don't be ridiculous. You have nothing I want or need."

"But your brother does. I believe he's giving you some sort of payment for my freedom. If I can show you the way to treble that amount, would you give me what I ask? A bigger house—just two extra rooms would do—and a servant. Compared with what you'd receive, it would be a drop in the ocean." She paused, watching the sparkle of greed grow in his bloodshot eyes, then added the extra hook that put her at risk. "In addition, if you win the bet, I will give myself to you for one month—to do with whatever you like."

Ah, she knew Midas too well. When she'd been his legal wife, he'd shown little interest in bedding her, but owning her as a slave to his whim would fire his desire. He would humiliate and abuse her to make up for having been coerced into setting her free.

"I'm listening." He leaned forward, gripping the arms of his throne.

Gwyneth drew a deep breath. Now that the moment was here, she was almost afraid to announce her plan. What if Ragnorak refused to participate, or what if he couldn't answer the questions she posed? What if, despite her seeming to place herself on the same side as Midas by her request for the bigger house, he suspected some kind of collusion and drew back?

"I will summon the Demon Lord here and now and ask three questions of him. If he can't answer the questions, I'll give myself to you as stated. If he can, the previous arrangement you made will be broken. You may not accept any more riches from the underworld yet you must still leave me and Brea alone."

Midas frowned. "You choose the questions? And you decide if the answers are right or wrong? How is that fair?"

"Three questions you agree to and the answers will be written down and kept in a sealed box." She gestured at the opulent room around them. "You're already wealthy, Highness. You have little to lose and even more to gain."

Midas rested his chin on his hand and tapped a finger against his lips, considering. Gwyneth was sure she'd struck the correct chord here. He loved people to notice and comment on his wealth. Her one anxiety was that he'd degenerated so far in recent months that he hadn't actually noticed how little he had left. Surely it couldn't be much.

Midas lifted his gaze. "Treble the riches and you and the child both return to the palace for a month."

"Not Brea. Only me." She wouldn't use her daughter as a bargaining tool, not even when she was almost certain she would win the bet. "And we get the house and servant."

He raised a hand. "Very well. Now, as to the questions..."

Gwyneth presented the three questions she had in mind and, after thinking about each one, Midas scoffed. "No man could answer such drivel. Only the first has an obvious answer. I'll give you that, because the others are so stupid I know he won't know the answers."

Thank God for the man's overwhelming greed that eclipsed his reason and for his low opinion of her mental faculties. It was astonishing he would accept her questions, but evidently she'd baited her hook carefully enough and now she must reel in her fish.

When Gwyneth's answers were locked in a box, it was time to summon the man who knew her better than anyone on this earth...or below it. She hadn't spoken his name aloud since she'd left Elohim, although she'd thought it often enough. Now she prayed the summoning power would work.

"Ragnorak, I need you," she whispered softly.

The air sizzled and, with a crack of thunder, Ragnorak appeared in their midst.

Chapter Nineteen

He heard his name murmured in his ear like a quiet caress, and Ragnorak knew instantly who called him. Gwyneth needed him. Perhaps she was in danger. Maybe Midas had changed his mind and thrown her into one of his dungeons to punish her for the gold-spinning lie. Or maybe, just maybe, she was pining for Ragnorak. Whatever the reason, he couldn't deny her call...and wouldn't have even if he'd had a choice. Like a magnet drawn to steel, he must go to Gwyneth though rock, fire, space or time itself might separate them.

He arrived in the throne room of the palace—thankfully clothed this time—to find it occupied only by Midas, his steward and a few guards, and Gwyneth. She was clothed in sky blue that made her astonishing eyes even brighter and her hair glow more golden than ever. For a moment, Ragnorak blocked all the other people in the room from his mind and concentrated solely on her. She smiled at him, and his blood burned like molten lava through his veins.

"You came." He'd forgotten how musical and sweet her voice sounded.

"Of course." Ragnorak bowed. "What do you need from me, my lady?"

She gazed fiercely into his eyes as if willing him to understand her as she proposed the terms of another contest.

"My lord Svartan, I'm not pleased you've had to sacrifice your kingdom's resources in order to preserve my freedom. I've suggested to King Midas he wager what you've promised him against the possibility of an even greater boon."

Ragnorak frowned and looked toward Midas, certain he'd put her up to this. "I'm satisfied with the terms we set."

"*I'm* not." Gwyneth said forcefully and took a step toward him. "I want my freedom free and clear or not at all."

"What do you propose, madam?"

"You will respond to three questions, the answers to which are in the sealed box which Wallace now holds." She indicated the steward. "If you answer correctly, Midas will release you from your debt, sign a permanent peace treaty between the upper and lower worlds, and write a binding promise that Brea and I will be forever free."

"And if I should answer incorrectly?" Ragnorak was already rejecting the plan in his mind. "What does he demand then?"

Descending the steps from the dais on which his throne stood, the king spoke at last. "Three times the yearly allotment you've promised and Gwyneth will return to the castle."

"No." He shook his head emphatically. "I stand by the previous bargain we struck. The answer is no."

"Svartan," Gwyneth spoke his name sharply, instantly drawing his attention back to her light. "You *must* make this deal. I have full confidence in your ability to answer the questions correctly. I'm staking my life on it."

"It's too dangerous. I would not put you at risk," he argued.

"It's my risk to take. In fact," she narrowed her eyes and spoke slowly, "*I* will make this bet. You promised once I could request any of the riches of your kingdom. Now I demand you fulfill that promise, but only if you lose the bet—which you won't."

"Gwyneth, you're being unreasonable." He strode toward her and stopped short of grasping her arms and shaking her. "There is no point to this bet. I'm satisfied to give Midas a little gold each year to keep you safe."

"There is a point." Her voice was quiet now, meant for his ears alone. "To prove how well you know me, like no other person ever has. We're meant to be together, Ragnorak, and after you answer these very easy questions, we'll find a way to arrange it. Both of us together. No more protestations that you're pushing me away for my own good as if I was some child."

Her eyes blazed the bright blue of lapis lazuli as she gazed into his. "Equals. Man and woman, husband and wife. We will find common ground and have our happily ever after. I insist on it."

At that moment, Ragnorak realized Gwyneth was a much more powerful being than he with all his rock shifting, air bending abilities. She was a goddess and he, her humble servant. But he didn't have to be happy about it.

He scowled. "Very well. Pose your questions."

Midas clapped his hands together. "Excellent. The bargain is struck. Begin."

Gwyneth folded her hands over her skirt, modestly covering the junction of her thighs as she asked a most immodest question. "What brings me to climax most quickly?"

A plethora of images flashed in Ragnorak's mind: Gwyneth with her head thrown back and her tender throat exposed, her face contorted in ecstasy, her pussy flushed and glistening before him, her hips thrusting, body rising and her cries as she achieved her goal. She was absolutely right. This was an easy question. He was surprised Midas had allowed it.

The king snorted. "I give you this one, Ragnorak. The

answer is so obvious."

Ragnorak spoke over him, offering his answer. "My tongue on your clit." In case her answer was more general, he amended, "Oral sex."

"Wrong!" Midas crowed with delight. "Every man knows women want only one thing in bed. Cock. That was so easy. I can't believe you missed it. Read the answer aloud, Wallace."

"Yes," Gwyneth agreed. "Break the seal and read the answer after each question rather than waiting until the end. Let there be no misunderstanding or reinterpretation of what was said here today."

Wallace swallowed hard as he opened the box and drew out the paper inside. From the grimness of his expression, Ragnorak guessed the man already knew the answer was correct—which said a little something about Wallace's prowess in the bedroom.

The steward cleared his throat before stammering, "The answer given is...oral s-sex."

"What? Let me see that?" Midas charged across the floor and snatched the paper from Wallace's hand. As he read, he frowned. "Ridiculous!'

"Your Highness, return the paper to Wallace," Gwyneth demanded boldly. "This is a fair contest. No lying or cheating on either side. To break the bargain would bring doom on the head of the person who dared interfere with the code of honor."

Midas's scowl deepened, but he thrust the paper back at the steward.

"My next question is this," Gwyneth continued. "What is the most precious thing between a man and a woman?"

"Hah! Not so easy now, is it, my would-be brother?" the king gloated. "Who knows what a woman imagines is important? It could be anything, their thoughts are so irrational."

Ragnorak considered. Midas was correct in that the question was a bit more challenging this time. Then he remembered lying quietly with Gwyneth after sex and simply breathing as they gazed into each other's eyes. He remembered the long talks and arguments they'd had, their shared laughter and their common worry over Brea's health when the baby had struggled for each breath. Remembering those moments made the answer quite obvious.

"Intimacy."

Absolute silence followed his pronouncement. The expressions on Midas and Wallace's faces—as well as the guards loitering near the door—were comical in their incredulity. Ragnorak nearly smiled, especially when he saw the twinkle in Gwyneth's eyes that let him know he'd answered correctly.

The nervous fear that had constricted his throat and made his heart pound began to alleviate as Ragnorak realized for the first time he had nothing to fear. He couldn't lose this bet. Gwyneth might as well have rigged it for she asked questions he couldn't get wrong—not with the way he knew the inner workings of her mind.

And also for the first time, he began to believe there was hope for a future for them together. She was right. They could find common ground, a way to make their worlds accommodate each of them.

When Wallace read the answer, "Intimacy," Midas stomped his foot on the floor.

"A lucky guess! But there's no way you'll know the answer to the last question. Even if she'd mentioned it before, you wouldn't remember such a foolish detail. No man would." The king didn't sound at all certain this time, and he made eye contact with the guards by the door.

Seeing the possibility of a double cross, Ragnorak casually moved closer to Gwyneth so he could grab her hand and take her with him if things went badly. The guards couldn't touch Ragnorak, but Midas might have instructed them to seize Gwyneth and use her as a tool to control him.

"My last question is silly yet simple." His lady smiled, and he knew he was home free. "What is my favorite kind of bird?"

Her laughter as she'd described her ongoing battle with the birds that lived under the eaves of her father's house rang in his head. He could hear her laughing, but couldn't for the life of him remember the type of bird. Mourning doves? Sparrows? Robins? Woodpeckers? His palms began to sweat and he clenched his fists by his sides. She should know he had little experience with birds, having lived his life underground.

But he looked into her eyes and Gwyneth's smile never faltered. She trusted him to remember. She believed he'd saved and stored every detail of their time together, every moment of conversation as well as every kiss. And, once more, of course she was right. Ragnorak delved deeper into his memory. He closed his eyes and relived the conversation they'd had as they strode the pathways of the Purple Caverns.

"One thing I miss down here—and I can't believe I'd ever miss them," she'd said, "is the horrible birds that used to leave their droppings on the floor of the porch back home. I don't know how many hours of my life I've spent, scrubbing those floorboards clean." She'd laughed. "Even so, I miss those wrens with their pretty red breasts and their annoying 'beeps'—such an unmusical bird call. But they were tiny and adorable and they had a nest of hatchlings every spring, which were amusing to watch."

"Wrens," Ragnorak nearly shouted. "Red breasted wrens are your favorite bird."

Gwyneth beamed while Wallace read in a faint voice,

"Wrens *is* the correct answer, sire."

Midas howled in fury. His face went bright red and twisted into a horrible mask of rage. He stomped his feet like a two-year-old throwing a tantrum and screamed, "It's not fair. He knew the answers already."

"You agreed to the questions," Gwyneth answered calmly. "The bet was fair and the results are binding. No more underworld riches for you to squander and no further contact between us."

"Guards!" the king yelled and the uniformed men moved forward.

Ragnorak reached for Gwyneth's hand, ready to whisk them both away, but he hesitated. A man who would break a deal, a man with a temper like Midas's, would never let the matter go. Gwyneth and Brea would be hunted. Elohim would be threatened. The people of the upper world would continue to suffer as long as Midas reigned. It was time to eliminate the problem.

Ragnorak strode toward his half-brother, took him by the hand and shook it firmly. "The deal is done. The bargain sealed. Truth and justice are revealed."

It was a simple incantation, but extremely effective. As Midas continued to stomp his feet against the floor, Ragnorak clung to his hand and pushed the power out of himself and into the very stones of the castle floor. In a mindless fury and seemingly unaware of the change in the air around him, Midas ranted and pounded his heels on the flagstones, which began to crackle and shift.

A glance at the guards told Ragnorak they'd fallen back, prudent self-preservation triumphing over obedience. The guards and the rat-faced steward remained in the room, silent witnesses to the king's destruction, but they looked ready to run out the door if necessary.

Ragnorak turned his concentration back to Midas. Neither judge nor executioner, he was merely a conduit for allowing the balancing power of the universe to bring Midas to his appropriate fate. He released the man's hand and watched as the evil king cursed and screamed at the guards to do his bidding, while continuing to jump up and down like a madman. With every stomp, the stones beneath his feet crumbled further, and suddenly they disintegrated completely. A pit opened. Deep within glowed orange flames which Ragnorak recognized as the molten lava of the earth's core, but knew the topsiders would perceive the fires of hell. It certainly didn't hurt to have humans fear the underworld in this way.

Awakening from his frenzy of fury, Midas stumbled backward, but it was too late. The vortex pulled at him with the suction of a tornado. He met Ragnorak's gaze for a fraction of a second. "Demon!" he shrieked and the word trailed away in a long, thin wail as he tumbled into the earth.

Epilogue

Gwyneth stepped out into the sunshine, Brea in her arms. Strolling across the terrace, she gazed out over the formal palace gardens to the woods spreading over the hills and into the distance. The trees were already changing to their warm, autumn colors, flashing red and gold in the morning sun. The breeze stirred her hair, tickled her cheeks. Everything reminded her of the joy of fresh air and sunlight.

Something landed with a splash beside her feet. A tiny bird dropping. Brea laughed with delight. Gwyneth turned her gaze upward to see a pair of wrens flying away from the palace roof.

"Even here," she murmured. But she smiled as she said it. Her heart was singing, because today at last he was coming for her.

And there were still some things to be done before she left. "Come, my little queen," she said into Brea's hair. "Time for you to get ready for Daddy while I do my final duty."

It wasn't final, of course. Just the last of this half-year. Going back inside, she saw the maid sweeping out the parlor corners.

"You won't forget to sweep and scrub the terrace, will you?" Gwyneth said a shade anxiously.

The maid ginned. "No, my lady. Have those little varmints been at it again?"

Gwyneth laughed. "Just one little varmint. But I know they'll be back. Thanks, Maria. I know I'll return to find everything just as we agreed."

"We'll miss you, my lady," the maid mumbled, bending back to her work.

Gwyneth smiled with just a hint of sadness. She'd miss this life, too. In the last few months, she'd made a real difference here. And not just in the palace, where everything now seemed so much brighter with heavy curtains thrown back, doors and windows open wide wherever possible, giving access to Brea's subjects as well as making the palace a far less oppressive place to live than in the bad old days of King Midas. The whole country seemed to have brightened with it. Trade had begun to flourish again. The harvest had been good. And unemployment was falling. No one now went hungry. Even the sick and destitute were cared for thanks to the sale of some of Midas's excessive treasure. And a little extra wealth from Elohim.

Gwyneth was proud of what they'd achieved here. She and Elohim's king, in the name of Queen Brea.

Giving her daughter into the willing care of her nurse, Gwyneth hurried to the council chamber. One more meeting, one more hour, and then *he* would be here. Excitement rose, as it still did whenever she thought of Ragnorak. She missed his embrace, his powerful, demanding loving. She missed his very presence. He'd been gone too long. Although this was, officially, their half-year above the ground, he'd had to spend the last week in Elohim attending to matters there and the parting had been hard on her.

The council were already gathered in the chamber and stood as she entered.

"Please, sit," she said at once, and as they did, she looked round at all of the familiar faces with something approaching affection. Even for Wallace, who, now that he had left his constant fear behind, had proven to be an able administrator. These were the men chosen by the Parliament—Brea's kingdom had taken the idea from Ragnorak's—as a sort of conduit between itself and the monarch. Which meant, until Brea came of age, herself and Ragnorak. They were also, largely, the men who had first come to her in the aftermath of Midas's death to offer Brea the crown, despite her gender, and Gwyneth the regency. The law was changed now to cover that, and the government was more stable than she could ever have dreamed of six months ago.

Against all the odds, she now trusted these men to run the kingdom well in her absence. With a satisfied nod, she sat and got down to business.

Less than an hour later, they had concluded everything they needed to discuss and agree upon. Slightly at a loss, Gwyneth rose to her feet.

"It seems there's nothing left to say except thank you—for your hard work and for your loyalty to my daughter. It does my heart good to see this kingdom begin to thrive at last. As it must lift yours to know you played so large a part in it."

Grandon, who bore the title of Prime Minister, stood, too, and bowed.

"It does," he acknowledged. "And to know that we were right to ask you to lead us. I won't deny we took a chance six months ago, that you, my lady, were the right person to guide us out of the chaos caused as much by the late king's rule as by his death, as we are now free to acknowledge. We remembered the good you managed to do in secret as queen, and came to you because of it. But I don't mind admitting now that our optimism was a shade desperate."

He gave a lopsided smile. "Or that our actions also had something to do with placating your formidable husband. Yet little more than half a year later, Parliament has asked me to convey to King Svartan its most sincere thanks for his considerable help in stabilizing and developing our country. We are aware—and grateful—that your regency is shared with him."

Oh, yes, they had come a long way from their fear of the demon king. It hadn't vanished, but it was masked by reluctant respect and admiration.

"I will pass on your kind words to the king," she said gravely. "And now..."

A sharp crack interrupted her, a rushing smell of smoke and faint sulphur assailed her nostrils and her heart jumped and soared.

Ragnorak, dressed in black as she'd first seen him, though without the mask, stepped out of the smoke.

Without thought, Gwyneth ran to him. They were to have met informally in their private chambers, but seeing him here, now, there was no way she could restrain her welcome to a languid offering of her hand to kiss. Somewhere, she was aware of the scraping of chairs as the council stood and bowed, but their politeness didn't receive the attention it deserved. Ragnorak's arms held her hard against his body, and she knew a secret thrill as the hard bulge of his erect cock pressed into her stomach.

"I missed you," he breathed into her mouth. But his kiss was quick and hard before he released her and turned to face the council. Almost with surprise, Gwyneth saw the bright figure of Karnak by his side. And yet they had discussed this, too.

"Gentlemen, you are already acquainted with my minister, Lord Karnak. As discussed, he is here to help you in any way he can, and to bring to us any matters you deem urgent. He can reach us immediately, so when the Lady Gwyneth and I depart with the queen, you are not deserted. We can return at any time we're needed."

His words were as much warning as comfort, and the council was aware of it. No matter how much trust had evolved between them, it was too early for Brea's position to be entirely safe, especially during a long absence. But Gwyneth could see no shuffling of feet or dropping of guilty eyes. She believed the council and the parliament would do their very best to make this work.

"And now," Ragnorak said in her ear. "It is time to go home." His voice promised so much more that she shivered with anticipation.

Brea's nurse tried very hard not to cry as they left her. Though the child kissed her when bidden, she grinned and waved with the casual callousness of the very young as Ragnorak spun the family through the vortex to Elohim.

They arrived not in the palace, but in the same underground caverns to which he had first brought them. Gwyneth blinked around her in surprise.

"Why here?" she asked. If it hadn't been for Brea's presence she would have suspected him of amorous intent. It was there in his burning eyes, in the grip of his caressing fingers on her arm.

But Ragnorak shrugged. "To apologize, perhaps. For the first time. I had wanted to dazzle you then with my world and its difference to your own. I never imagined it would appall you."

"It doesn't anymore," she said, almost surprising herself with the perfect truth of her statement. "I was frightened and too angry to see the beauty. But I learned to, during those weeks with you."

His hand slid up her arm to her shoulder. "Then you didn't

just agree to live here for part of the year to please me?"

Gwyneth rubbed her cheek on his hand. "No," she admitted. "I haven't been here since you sent me away but...I associate it with you..." She cast him a mischievous glance. "...and with love."

His breath caught. "I'll do my best to live up to that. Just as soon as I get you alone."

"Then we'd better tell you Brea's news at once."

"What news is this?"

His eyes flew quickly between Gwyneth and the child, who lunged at him, with grasping hands and big smiles. Normally Gwyneth would have happily relinquished her into Ragnorak's arms, but this time she turned away from him and let Brea slide to the rocky ground.

"Stand back three paces," Gwyneth ordered, and when Ragnorak obeyed, she whispered in Brea's ear: "Walk to Daddy." And Brea pulled against her hands. Gwyneth let go and the child set off toward him with small, erratic and none too steady steps.

Ragnorak caught her up in his arms, swinging her high and telling her how clever she was. "And I missed it!" he exclaimed. "One week away, and I missed her first steps!"

"It was bad timing," Gwyneth agreed sympathetically as her daughter hugged him. "But you're still only the second person to see it. Even her nurse doesn't know. I kept it for you."

Ragnorak's eyes softened, but what he would have said remained a mystery as Agnet and three male palace servants appeared just then from a cavern on the right. To Gwyneth's surprise, Agnet ran to her, seizing her hand and pressing it fervently to her lips, then standing back to grin widely at her. Almost as if she was too pleased for words.

Gwyneth felt her own smile rise in response, but before she

could speak, Ragnorak said, "I asked them to meet us here and take Brea to the palace. We'll join her there shortly."

Doubtfully, Gwyneth handed her daughter over, wondering if she'd be content with a stranger. After all, it was very unlikely she would remember Agnet. But whether she remembered or not, Brea seemed very interested in Agnet's face and bright necklace, and when Ragnorak said they would see her soon, she simply nodded and gave her attention to her new friend.

Slightly piqued by the ease of her daughter's affections, Gwyneth shrugged and watched as the palace party walked away along the colorful stone passage. Brea even waved to her. Gwyneth waved back, and then they were out of sight.

"She will be all right down here," Ragnorak said anxiously. "We agreed her illness was probably *not* caused by our atmosphere."

"No, I don't think it was. She can get ill anywhere, proven by the sniffles she had last month, and I'm happiest when you're close by to heal her. I think she likes it here." She glanced up at Ragnorak. "Where are we going?"

"Come," said Ragnorak. He took her hand and they began to walk.

"I've been here before," Gwyneth said when he paused at last. Water fell from the rocks above, rushed along in bubbling streams when it hit the cavern floor. She melted as she remembered. Ragnorak crouched down in the very place he had once seduced her to willingness and then taken nothing. His long, sensitive fingers brushed along the rock, tracing the tiny humps and valleys.

"It was here," said Ragnorak, "that I first thought I might be winning you. I used to come to this place as a boy to think and dream in peace. Sometimes, I used to imagine bringing a woman here, a special woman, and making love to her until she loved me truly for myself instead of my power." He gave a quick, deprecating smile. "I am, you see, as subject to self-pity as the next man."

"No you're not." She knelt facing him. "And there's no crime in loneliness. I didn't trust you when you brought me here the first time, but I already loved you."

He touched her cheek. "Really? And I hadn't even made love to you. Not here."

She swallowed as heat flooded her body. "Something tells me that's about to change," she said huskily, and reached up to kiss him.

At the first meeting of their lips, desire exploded between them. Kneeling opposite her, he tugged up her skirts and reached underneath without further preamble. And yet there was nothing coarse about his action. It seemed the most natural thing in the world that his wonderful, caressing hand should slide up her naked thigh to her aching pussy and claim it. Bathing his fingers in her wetness, he gave a groan that was more than half triumph.

"Then you missed me, too."

She gave a sob of laughter into his mouth. His fingers fumbled between their bodies at his fastenings. His hand left her pussy to grasp his own cock, and she broke the kiss to watch as he guided his big, rigid shaft between her thighs.

She moaned again as it slid between her folds. It glided over her clitoris, and the pleasure was like a lightening flash. Then he entered her body, and Ragnorak gave a sigh, as if he had come home. But he stayed unmoving inside her, as if having sunk into her at last, his hurry was over and he had all the time in the world. He kissed her again and began to undress her.

"What if someone comes past?" she whispered against his lips.

"I don't care. This is one loving no one will interrupt."

"Then we'd better be quick," Gwyneth pleaded, not without ulterior motive as his thumb tortured one naked nipple in slow, aching spirals.

Ragnorak bent his mouth to the other, taking it between his lips and rolling it. Gwyneth thrust forward involuntarily, and his hand covered her now naked bottom to hold her there, hard against him while his still cock throbbed inside her and his hand and mouth ravished her breast.

"Quick?" he repeated, pausing to lick at her hard, excited nipple. "Only when *I* decide." With that, he took both her hands, placing them behind her back and only then began to thrust with agonizing slowness, "I like to have you naked and helpless in my power."

"You would shame me before your people?" she gasped.

He raised his head and looked at her seriously. "Do you feel ashamed?"

He was quite still once more. But though her pussy begged to be fucked, she did him the courtesy of thinking about his question.

A choked laugh broke from her throat. "No," she confessed. "And besides, I don't believe you've left anything to chance. The ways are blocked, aren't they?"

Ragnorak smiled and, with clear purpose, laid her on her back. He loomed over her, dark, awesome, but very far from frightening to her now. Love curled around the desire in her belly, the force of it making her want to weep and laugh and shout at the same time. She contented herself with winding her arms around his neck.

He said, "It seems you know me too well, too. How am I to make this constantly exciting for you if you guess the reality behind my fantasies?"

"Just do some more of that," she whispered, succumbing to the soaring pleasure as he thrust into her repeatedly. "And then we can...go home and be...good."

"Well, we can go home," he allowed breathlessly, pausing to grind his cock against her pulsing clitoris. She let out a whimper and arched into him, squeezing. "I have something special for you tonight."

The very idea of receiving anything more special than the exquisite pleasure of the present was enough to push Gwyneth over the edge.

"Oh, Ragnorak," she gasped, in the sweetest of all summonses. "Oh, my demon, *come*!"

About the Author

To learn more about Bonnie Dee, please visit bonniedee.com. Send an email to her at bondav40@yahoo.com or join her Yahoo! group to join in the fun with other readers as well as Bonnie. groups.yahoo.com/group/bonniedee. You can reach Bonnie on Twitter: http://twitter.com/Bonnie_Dee, or Facebook:
http://www.facebook.com/album.php?profile=1&id=1352577313

To learn more about Marie Treanor, please visit www.marietreanor.com. Send an email to Marie at marie@marietreanor.com or join her Yahoo! group to join in the fun with other readers as well as Marie! groups.yahoo.com/group/sexydelights. Subscribe to Marie's Newsletter at groups.yahoo.com/group/marietreanornewsletter.

Three balls. Three sexual adventures. One true love.

Cinderella Unmasked

© 2009 Bonnie Dee and Marie Treanor

Fairytale Fantasies

In the years since her husband King Charming boarded a pirate ship to "find himself", Queen Ella has ruled alone. Romantic love? It's a girlish emotion. These days, her only confidant is her steward, Sebastian.

Five years is a long time to forego sexual pleasures. She's the queen, after all. Shouldn't she be allowed a few indulgences? A masquerade is just the ticket to find fulfillment Charming never gave her. With Sebastian's encouragement—and a little help from a fairy godmother—Ella prepares to make some magic.

The first masked stranger she dallies with gives her a taste of what she's been craving. And it's just not enough. A second ball follows. A third. Each one—and each anonymous man—sends her to new heights of sexual pleasure. And reawakens the notion that maybe, just maybe, love does not always lead to pain.

Her indiscretions have not gone unnoticed. As her stepfamily makes a move to take over the throne, Ella has nowhere to turn, no one to trust...except the men behind the masks...

Warning: This is the new *"happily ever after", strictly for grown-ups...*

LaVergne, TN USA
16 February 2011
216725LV00011B/8/P

9 781609 280147